RIDING THE STORM

Jody felt a clutch of apprehension in her stomach. Isn't it good sailing weather?' she asked.

'It is right now,' Matt agreed. 'We made record time! But haven't you heard the warnings?'

'Warnings?' she repeated weakly.

'All sailors are being told to seek shelter,' Matt replied. 'There's a major tropical storm brewing. Winds of over a hundred miles per hour predicted. There's no way anyone with any sense would want to be out at sea today!'

Look out for more titles in this series

Dolphin Diaries™

RIDING THE STORM
Lucy Daniels

Hodder
Children's
Books

a division of Hodder Headline

Special thanks to Lisa Tuttle

**Thanks also to Dr Horace Dobbs of
International Dolphin Watch for reviewing the
dolphin information in this book**

First published in Great Britain in 2000
by Hodder Children's Books

A Catalogue record for this book is available from the British Library

ISBN 0 340 77859 8

Typeset by Avon Dataset Ltd, Bidford-on-Avon, Warks

Printed and bound in Great Britain by
Clays Ltd, St Ives plc

Hodder Children's Books
a division of Hodder Headline
338 Euston Road
London NW1 3BH

1

July 15 – mid-morning.
Atlantic Spotted Dolphins!

My first sighting of Stenella frontalis. *We were still eating breakfast when Cam gave a shout from on deck. I went racing up to see. There were four of them swimming very close together, and they came right up to the side of the boat. When Dad and I leaned over to look, they poked their heads out of the water and looked right back at us! Their backs were an almost purplish colour under the masses of white spots, with lighter sides and whitish underneath. In size and shape they seemed a lot like the bottlenose dolphins I've known, and every bit as friendly, fast and playful. But they didn't stick around for very long . . .*

Jody McGrath sighed and leaned back in her bunk, letting her pen and diary fall into her lap. The latest dolphin sighting had been exciting, but all too brief. *Dolphin Dreamer* had left Key West nearly a week earlier, heading for the Bahamas, and the days at sea had been long, slow and uneventful.

Sean and Jimmy, Jody's mischievous twin brothers, were being especially troublesome today. She had come down to her cabin to escape their pestering, but, now that she had brought her diary up to date, she didn't know what to do with herself.

Back home in Fort Lauderdale, she would have picked up the phone and called her best friend Lindsay. The thought gave her a pang of loneliness. She longed for someone to talk to. Instead, she picked up her diary again . . .

Sometimes I feel so stuck on this boat! I wonder what Lindsay's doing now? She promised she would e-mail me every day, but it's been nearly a week since her last message. Maria and Devon haven't answered my last e-

mails, either. I have this horrible feeling that they're all out having fun together and have forgotten about me completely . . .

Tears welled up and she had to stop writing and grope for a tissue.

'What's wrong with you?' The voice was loud and impatient.

Jody was startled. She had been too caught up in her own thoughts to notice her bunk-mate entering the cabin. Brittany, daughter of Harry Pierce, *Dolphin Dreamer*'s English captain, stood staring at her, looking unfriendly, as usual. She was the one person on board who had nothing to do with the Dolphin Universe project and didn't want to be there. However, she'd been left by her mother in her father's care at the last minute, and with no one else to look after her, she'd had to come along.

'Nothing,' Jody said hastily. She turned to stow away her diary and quickly wiped her eyes.

'You were crying. I saw you,' Brittany persisted. She sat down on Jody's bunk. 'Tell me what you were crying about.' She still didn't sound that friendly, but it was obvious she expected an answer.

'I was just feeling kind of homesick,' Jody

confessed. She didn't expect any sympathy, and she was right.

'You!' Brittany sounded disbelieving. 'How could you be homesick? You're right here with your whole family, and you've told me about a million times how much you love being part of this dumb dolphin research project! Nobody forced you to leave home and live with a bunch of strangers – what have *you* got to cry about?'

'I miss my friends,' Jody replied. She bit her lip as tears threatened again. How different things would be if she was sharing this cabin with Lindsay, instead of with spoiled, unfriendly Brittany!

Brittany's expression softened. 'So do I,' she said quietly. 'I miss hanging out at the mall with the other kids. And I miss my own bedroom, and my own computer, and watching TV, and our swimming-pool . . .' A yearning look came over her face. 'But mostly I miss my mom.' She looked directly at Jody, leaning confidingly close. 'It's just so awful not hearing from her, not even knowing if she's gotten any of my messages. I need to talk to her. Can I use your computer to e-mail her again? Please?'

Jody's heart sank. She really did sympathise with Brittany's desperation, especially as she'd been feeling lonely, too. She couldn't imagine her own mother flying off to another country without even telling her when she'd be back! But they'd been through this before. 'You know we have to ask my parents before going on-line while we're at sea,' she replied, as gently as she could. 'Phone calls and computer link-ups have to go by satellite, and that costs a ton of money.'

Brittany frowned impatiently. 'This is important! Just let me check my e-mail – I'll be on line for less than a minute. My dad will pay for it!'

Jody knew that Harry had tried to contact his ex-wife by phone and e-mail many times already. 'Maybe you'd better ask your dad, then,' she said. 'I wanted to check my e-mail last night, but Mom told me to wait till we reach Port Lucaya. It won't be long . . .'

Tension had been building in Brittany as she listened. Now she snapped. 'Thanks a lot! You wouldn't have to tell your mom what I'd done! You're such a goody-goody, Jody McGrath, I don't know how you can stand yourself!' With that, Brittany stormed out of the cabin.

Jody winced. It was so unfair to be blamed for things that weren't her fault – but that was just typical of Brittany. She waited a minute, so Brittany wouldn't think she was following her, and then left the cabin.

Jody's parents, Craig and Gina McGrath, were in the saloon with Harry Pierce, looking at a navigation chart spread out on the table. Brittany was nowhere to be seen.

'*Honey Bee* should be on Little Bahama Bank, right about here,' Craig said, tapping the chart with his finger.

'What's *Honey Bee?*' Jody asked curiously, going to join her parents.

Her mother smiled and put an arm around her. 'That's the name of Matt Anderson's catamaran – his boat.'

Jody recognised the man's name. 'You mean Dad's old friend from college?'

Craig nodded. 'That's right. Matt came out here straight after graduation to pursue his own research. He's been studying the same group of dolphins for more than a dozen years – he's an expert on the Atlantic spotted dolphin, and he's built up a huge database,' he went on enthusiastically.

'Sounds perfect to add to the Dolphin Universe database,' Jody said. 'I can't wait to meet him.'

'Don't you mean, you can't wait to meet his dolphins?' Her father's blue eyes twinkled as he gave her a teasing smile.

Jody grinned back. 'Mind-reader! So when does this happen?'

'I've just made radio contact, and he's given us his coordinates,' Craig told her.

'We're already on course,' said Harry from across the table. He straightened up. 'I'll need to check the wind-speed, but at a guess, we should be approaching *Honey Bee* in about half an hour.'

'Matt said his boat is right in the middle of a large, friendly group of Atlantic spotted dolphins at this very moment,' her father added.

'Great!' said Jody. 'I hope they stick around till we get there!' She felt excitement rising like bubbles inside her. The last few days at sea had been a bit too quiet for Jody. But now that was going to change. 'I'm going up on deck,' she said eagerly. 'Maybe I'll be the first to see them!'

Her mother gave her a quick hug and let her go. 'You watch out for pirates, now,' she said mysteriously.

Jody understood what her mother had meant as soon as she emerged on deck and caught sight of her twin brothers.

Sean was wearing an eye-patch and a painted-on curling black moustache. He was standing with his hands on his hips. Jimmy, with a red bandana tied around his head, was brandishing a cardboard sword. 'You'll walk the plank for that, matey!' he roared at his brother.

Jody rolled her eyes. She wished she had someone to share her feelings with and thought again, with a pang, of Lindsay. Why couldn't Brittany have been somebody nicer, somebody she could have been friends with?

She looked at Cameron Tucker, the second mate, who was at the helm while the captain was below. 'I hope these pesky pirates aren't bothering you, Cam,' she said.

He shrugged and winked at her. 'Just one of the hazards of sailing in the Caribbean,' he said. 'I've seen worse.'

'You've never seen worse pirates than us,' Jimmy objected. 'We're the worstest pirates that ever there was!'

'Yeah – the worst eight-year-old pirates,' Jody replied. She went to lean against the side, as far away from her brothers as she could get, and gazed out at the sparkling blue waves. The sun blazed down out of a clear blue sky, as it had every day that week, but the wind that now filled the sails also kept them cooler

Sean and Jimmy fooling around – as usual!

than they would have been on shore. As always, Jody scanned the surface of the water, searching for a curved fin, or a splash, or the wonderful sight of a glistening, streamlined body leaping joyfully into the air. But there was nothing to disturb the endless waves of the sea around them.

From behind her, Jody heard one of her brothers shout, 'You're my prisoner!'

Then Maddie's voice, sounding cool and amused, said, 'Do you know who you're talking to? I'm nobody's prisoner – I'm the Queen of the Pirates, and I've just comandeered this vessel!'

Jody turned to watch. Maddie was her parents' assistant, but before she'd decided to study marine biology she had worked as an elementary school teacher. Maybe that was why she could handle Jody's younger brothers so well.

Sean scowled, screwing up his one visible eye. 'Girls can't be pirates,' he objected.

Maddie's eyes widened disbelievingly. 'Don't tell me you've never heard of Anne Bonney? Or Mary Read?'

Sean looked at Jimmy, who shrugged.

'For real?' Sean asked Maddie.

She nodded solemnly. 'Nearly three hundred years

ago, Mary Read, Anne Bonney, and her pirate husband Calico Jack, sailed in these very waters making daring raids on merchant ships.'

Jody found herself getting interested, even though she thought her brothers' pirate obsession was silly.

The boys were fascinated, bombarding Maddie with questions:

'Where?'

'What was the pirate ship called?'

'Did they bury their treasure?'

Maddie laughed and held up her hands in surrender. 'Come below and I'll tell you everything. Your mom says you've been playing out in the hot sun long enough.'

When they had gone, Jody leaned over the side again. The water was very clear here, and seemed quite shallow. She could see right down to the soft white sandy bottom. It was easy to imagine herself down there, gliding effortlessly through the water, as free and easy as a wild dolphin . . .

'*Ship ahoy!*' Her father's voice, amplified by the loud-hailer, boomed out in the quiet air, rousing Jody from her dreams.

'Ahoy, *Honey Bee!*' As Craig spoke into the loud-hailer again, Jody straightened up and hurried over to the other side of the deck where her parents were standing. They were approaching a twin-hulled boat with yellow sails. There was a crowd of people on board, most of them gazing down into the water.

Jody gasped as she saw what they were looking at. In the water around *Honey Bee*, there must have been at least twenty dolphins bobbing, diving and frolicking.

Cam was busy dashing about, hauling in the sails to slow *Dolphin Dreamer*'s speed while the captain changed course.

Craig raised the loud-hailer and spoke again. 'Request permission to approach!'

Another amplified voice came echoing across the water. 'Ahoy, *Dolphin Dreamer*! Permission granted! Welcome aboard! What took you so long?'

Craig chuckled. 'Good old Matt,' he said fondly.

Jody grinned and hugged herself with excitement as their boat drew nearer to *Honey Bee* and the crowd of dolphins. Unlike the bottlenose dolphins she knew, the Atlantic spotted dolphins had obvious differences between them. Some had lots of distinct spots, some had only a few; the spots were clear and separate on some, and blurred together on others; even their colours were different. It was going to be easier to recognise and keep track of this group than the bottlenose dolphins, and she couldn't wait to get to know them.

But, as they drew nearer still, the dolphins began to leave. At first, only a few swam away, but soon, as if the word had spread quickly, all the dolphins took off, swimming rapidly away from both boats.

Jody stared after them in dismay. 'What's wrong?' she asked her parents. 'Why are they all leaving? Did we scare them?'

Her father looked as concerned as she felt. 'I don't know, honey,' he said slowly. 'I hope not, but . . . it certainly looks that way.'

From the other boat there came a buzz of disappointed voices, cries of 'Come back!' and whistles which seemed to be attempts at the dolphins' own sounds. But the dolphins responded to none of it. Within minutes, they had all vanished from sight, as if they had never been there.

2

'I'm really sorry if we scared off your dolphins,' Craig said after they'd boarded *Honey Bee* and he'd introduced Maddie, Jody and the twins to his old friend Matt.

Matt Anderson was a tall, thin, deeply tanned man with a long, friendly face. 'It's not your fault,' he assured Craig, including the whole group with his quick, warm smile. 'The dolphins are just kind of wary of strange boats right now, that's all. Stick around for a while, and they'll come back.'

'Actually, we *were* hoping to stick around for a while, to see what you're up to,' Craig replied. 'But the captain and crew would like to get into port pretty soon, to take care of business. Mei Lin, our cook, is desperate to buy some fresh fruit and vegetables. But if you don't mind, we could stay here with you on *Honey Bee* for a few hours, and then Harry could sail back to pick us up—'

'They don't have to come back for you,' Matt interrupted. 'We're spending the afternoon out here observing dolphins, then sailing into Port Lucaya in time to have dinner, so we'll take you back.'

Gina, Maddie and Jody all nodded enthusiastically when Craig looked at them.

He grinned. 'That sounds great,' he told Matt. 'I'll tell Harry that we're staying and he can go.'

Suddenly, Maddie gave a gasp, her eyes wide.

'What's wrong, Maddie?' asked Gina.

'We forgot somebody,' Maddie replied softly.

Jody thought that Maddie must mean Brittany. 'Oh, Brittany's sure to want to go into the port with Harry and Cam and Mei Lin,' she said.

Maddie shook her head. 'Who else?' she prompted.

Then they got it. Craig groaned, Gina laughed, and Jody named the person they'd nearly forgotten: 'Dr Taylor!'

Dr Jefferson Taylor was a scientist who worked for PetroCo, the oil company that was providing much of the funding for Dolphin Universe. The funding had come with a catch, though: PetroCo had insisted that Dr Taylor came along as part of the research team. He was on board to get good publicity for the oil company, showing that they were interested in dolphin conservation. But so far, Dr Taylor had not proved to be much use as a dolphin research scientist!

'I'd better go find him,' Craig said with a sigh. 'He'd never forgive us otherwise.'

Jody noticed that her brothers were talking to a boy who looked about eight or nine. 'Is that your son?' she asked Matt.

For a moment Matt looked startled. 'No, I don't have any children – my girlfriend Anna hasn't even agreed to marry me yet! Why, do you think he looks like me?'

Jody felt herself blushing slightly at the misunderstanding. The boy was sturdily built, with very pale blond hair, and looked nothing at all like the lean, dark man smiling down at her. 'No. Only, he's too young to be a crew-member, so I thought he must be family.'

'Oh, of course,' Matt said kindly. 'No, he's neither crew nor family – he's here with his parents. They're tourists, like the rest of the people on board today –

apart from my assistant Adam. That's how I finance my research: people pay to come out on *Honey Bee* to learn about dolphins, and even get to know them a little.'

'That sounds great!' Jody exclaimed enthusiastically.

Matt smiled again. 'Glad you think so. Come and meet everybody – I see your brothers have got a head start on that already!'

Matt introduced the boy Sean and Jimmy were talking to as Logan Schroeder. He and his parents were visiting from Colorado. The rest of the tour members were Anita and Kim Lapidus, a mother and her teenage daughter from Florida; Bob and Kathy Moran, an elderly couple from Vermont; and Jim and Megan Hobb, from Texas.

Adam Jones, Matt's assistant, was from nearby Freeport. He seemed a quiet young man with a sweet smile.

'Excuse me, Mr Anderson, but do you think that the dolphins will come back today?' Logan asked. Everyone waited intently to hear Matt's reply.

'I hope so, Logan,' Matt said. 'I'm going to put some special music on – it often attracts them when they hear it playing from the underwater speakers. The boat our friends arrived on is about to leave, and once it's gone there shouldn't be any reason for the dolphins to stay away. They know they have nothing to fear from anyone on *Honey Bee*.'

Jody frowned. Matt had said that it wasn't their fault, yet it sounded as if their arrival *had* scared off the dolphins – but why? Dolphins were not timid creatures, and were usually curious about the boats they met.

Jimmy obviously thought the same thing, because he spoke up loudly. 'They don't have to be scared of *Dolphin Dreamer*. We *love* dolphins. And we've got lots of dolphin friends back in Florida to prove it!'

There were chuckles from a few of the adults.

'I'm sure you do, Jimmy,' Matt said. 'And once the dolphins of Little Bahama Bank get to know you, I'm sure they'll love you, too. The problem isn't with *Dolphin Dreamer*, but another boat, called *Stormrider*, and the obnoxious college kids who've chartered her for their summer break.' He looked very serious. 'A lot of people don't understand the damage a motor-boat can do to a dolphin. They haven't seen a curious dolphin get badly cut by a propellor. I have.'

Jody caught her breath, shocked.

'Those guys are worse than that,' said Jim Hobb with a frown. 'Ignorant is one thing – cruel is another.

We've run into them before. They think it's funny to tease and torment animals.'

Matt nodded. 'I'm afraid Jim is right,' he said. 'I was told they even caught one dolphin in a net, and although they let it go, it must have been a terrifying experience for the poor creature. Anyway, the result is that just lately, the local dolphins are getting a bit nervous whenever a strange boat turns up.'

Listening to this, Jody was horrified. She knew that not everyone shared her passion for dolphins, but how could anyone want to hurt such wonderful animals? 'Who are they?' she demanded.

Matt shrugged. 'Some brats with more money than sense. They really should know better.'

Just then, Craig arrived with Dr Taylor, who was looking distinctly rumpled and sleepy-eyed. He yawned as he was introduced to Matt Anderson, and then apologised, sounding rather sorry for himself. 'Excuse me, Dr Anderson, but I wasn't expecting this meeting. It *is* siesta time, you know . . .'

'Ah, yes, the wonderful Spanish tradition of a nap in the afternoon,' Matt replied politely. 'We've got too much going on to want to stop for siesta on *Honey Bee*, but there are bunks down below if you'd like . . .'

'No, no,' Dr Taylor said quickly, waving his hand.

'Of course I'll fit in with what everyone else wants to do! I'm always glad to meet fellow scientists and learn about their work. Er, what *is* your work, exactly?'

Just then Jody heard Logan give a glad cry: 'The dolphins! They're coming back!'

Jody rushed to join her brothers and Logan at the side of the boat. A herd of spotted dolphins, at least nine or ten of them, was swimming rapidly in their direction.

Logan leaned eagerly over the side. 'Look! Look, there's Cressy. And that's Debby – she's real friendly. And see the little one without any spots? That's her calf, Dobbin. He'll be one year old next month. Matt told us he got to see Dobbin when he was just born.'

'Why doesn't he have any spots?' Jody asked, surprised. 'His mother is covered in them!' Debby's spots were so numerous they blurred together and looked more like several large patches.

'Oh, that's 'cause he's just a baby,' Logan explained. 'They're born without any spots at all, and only start getting them when they're about four years old. They get more and more every year, and when they get old the spots all run together into one huge gigantic blur.'

'That sort of pattern helps us know how old they are,' said Matt, coming up behind them. 'But the way

21

their appearance changes from year to year makes it really hard to keep tabs on who's who, unless they've got a scar or some other permanent mark.'

'Just like the bottlenose dolphins,' said Jody. She thought of Rosie, a young dolphin she had got to know in the Florida Keys. A knot of scar tissue over one eye, where she'd once been snagged by a fish-hook, had made her easy to recognise.

'Anyone fancy a swim?' asked Matt.

Jody whirled around and gazed up at him. 'Really? You mean we can go in with them?'

Matt cocked his head and looked down at the dolphins swimming close beside the stationary boat. 'Yeah, it looks to me like those guys want company.' He grinned at Jody and her brothers. 'I hope you kids brought your swimsuits!' When they nodded eagerly, he said, 'Maybe Logan will show you where to get changed.'

'You guys are in for a big treat,' said Logan as they hurried down below to change. 'This is the best vacation I've ever had. My folks think so, too. Swimming with wild dolphins is just . . . the best . . .'

'Yeah, we know,' said Jimmy, affecting a bored attitude. 'We do it all the time.'

'Oh, sure.' Logan grinned, disbelieving.

'We do so,' Jimmy insisted.

'Not *all* the time,' Jody corrected him. 'We've only swum with bottlenose dolphins a few times. You see,' she explained to the open-mouthed Logan, 'our parents' job is to study dolphins. We live on a boat and we just go wherever the dolphins are.' Then, hoping to make him feel better, she added, 'But we've never been swimming with Atlantic spotted dolphins before!'

They were soon ready to go into the water along with Kim and her mother, Logan's parents, the Hobbs, and Gina. The elderly couple decided they would just watch from the deck and take photographs.

Matt was also going to stay on the boat to bring Craig and Dr Taylor up to date on his work. He explained that if there were more people than dolphins in the water, the dolphins would probably leave. 'We don't want to overwhelm them,' he said. 'We like to keep things equal, so everybody has fun.'

'I'll stay on board, too,' Maddie volunteered. 'That way, I can video everything that's going on below.'

'That's great, Maddie, thanks,' said Gina warmly.

Matt looked over the group assembled on deck and grinned. 'I can see you're all ready now, and I know you're all experienced, so I won't go through the whole drill this time. But just to be sure – what're the two most important things to remember when swimming with dolphins?'

Logan's hand shot up. When Matt gave him a nod, he said, 'Don't grab!'

'Absolutely right,' Matt agreed. 'Until a dolphin gets to know and trust you, even the friendliest touch could seem like a threat. Don't even reach out to them. Let them come to you, if they want to. The second thing?'

'Don't cover their blowhole?' Sean suggested, giving his brother a sideways look. Jimmy had once got into trouble for doing that.

'You got it,' Matt said with a smile. 'OK, end of lecture. Have some fun!'

Gina grabbed the twins before they could get away. 'No war-cries, boys,' she informed them sternly. 'And no yelling.'

Jimmy looked crestfallen. 'So we can't be pirates?'

'Play something quieter,' his mother advised.

'I know,' said Sean. He jabbed his brother in the arm. 'We'll be sharks. Silent, but deadly!'

Jimmy's face lit up. 'Yeah, cool!' he agreed.

Jody slipped over the side and into the water. It felt absolutely wonderful, even warmer and calmer than the ocean off the coast of Florida. It was also the clearest water she had ever seen, so bright and transparent it was like nothing at all. The brilliant white sand on the bottom, less than ten metres down, reflected the sun so brightly it was like having another light shining upwards. Everything in the water, even her own arms and legs, seemed to gleam and sparkle.

She looked around at everyone else and thought that it was like being in a swimming-pool in the ocean – except that most swimming-pools didn't have dolphins in them!

The nearness of the dolphins almost took Jody's breath away. And there were so many of them! She remembered seeing nine or ten approaching *Honey Bee*, but more must have arrived when she wasn't looking. There might have been as many as twenty, but it was impossible to count as they kept moving.

It was like an ocean party. People were laughing and murmuring to the dolphins, and the dolphins gently clicked and whistled back. There was even music floating out of the underwater speakers – Jody's mother told her it was Handel's *Water Music*, and she thought that was the perfect choice!

A trio of lightly spotted dolphins suddenly glided past, so close Jody could almost reach out and touch them. She gazed down through the crystal-clear water and saw them flip over and swim back towards her, this time on their backs. Were they inviting her to play? Jody swam after them, trying to imitate their movements, but when they dived down to the bottom, to balance on their noses on the white sand, she had to give up. Perhaps she could have joined them if she'd had diving gear on, but that would just have to wait for another time.

Suddenly Jody noticed two dolphins together, one bigger than the other. The bigger one was heavily spotted; the smaller one had no spots at all, just a purplish-black back which faded to grey on the sides, and a white belly. Although this was not the pair that Logan had pointed out from the boat, Jody was certain that this was another mother and calf. They seemed interested in her, so she swam closer. When she was only inches away, she stopped.

The two dolphins lay almost still in the water, facing her. The calf was underneath its mother, cuddling under her fin.

Jody smiled: it looked so sweet! Then she saw something that surprised her. The mother had some sort of little fish on her back. It was about six inches long, and it was moving. Jody couldn't tell if it was

Me and some spotted dolphins!

crawling or swimming, but as she watched, the little creature made its way along the dolphin's back and down her side, to settle just above one of her fins. Now Jody could see that the fish seemed to be *attached* to the dolphin in some way – it had some sort of sucker or something on its head. She wondered if the dolphin knew it was there, and if she minded.

She had been so still while she was watching that the baby dolphin lost all nervousness and came away from its mother to investigate this new visitor. It swam right up to Jody and then swam all around her, coming as close as possible without actually touching her. Jody held still, not wanting to frighten it, but then she heard a cry from someone else:

'Oh, look, there's a baby one – isn't it cute!'

Suddenly there were two or three people swimming in their direction. It was too much for the calf, which scooted back to its mother in alarm. She immediately swam rapidly away, shepherding her calf to a safer distance.

Jody felt disappointed, but not for long. There were plenty of other dolphins around, lots to look at, think about and do. Time went by swiftly. She could hardly believe it when it was time to get out. Only as she pulled herself up the ladder back onto *Honey Bee* and felt the trembling in her arms and legs did she realise that she really had been swimming for long enough!

Everyone sat around on the deck, snacking on dried fruit and nuts, candy bars, and soft drinks while they shared their experiences. Jody told about the odd little fish she'd seen attached to the mother dolphin. 'What could it have been?' she asked.

'It's called a remora,' Matt said. 'Sometimes known as a suckerfish.'

'I've seen that dolphin too!' Logan exclaimed.

'Yes, Mary seems to be especially drawn to younger people since she became a mother,' Matt said.

'Why do you call her Mary?' Jody asked curiously.

Matt grinned. 'Mary and her little lamb,' he explained. 'Everywhere that Mary went, the lamb was sure to go!'

'So you call the calf "Lamb"?' Jody guessed. It sounded odd to her, since the calf wouldn't always need its mother that much.

Matt laughed. 'No, no,' he said. 'The calf is known as Skipper ! It's the remora that is her lamb. Nobody knows why some dolphins have them when most don't, but those who do, tend to keep them for years – as if they were pets.'

Dr Taylor snorted loudly. 'That's quite ridiculous! Animals don't keep pets. The remora is a parasite, and that's all,' he declared.

'What's a parasite?' Jimmy demanded.

'It's a creature that lives off another animal,' Gina explained quietly. 'Like a flea or a tick on a dog.'

Dr Taylor frowned and shook his head at Matt. 'Would you say that a dog with fleas was keeping lots of pets? It's bad enough to see a scientist having to work as a tour guide, but to hear a man with a PhD telling such sentimental stories to tourists is disgraceful.'

Jody held her breath and looked quickly at Matt to see how her father's friend would take this sudden attack.

Matt kept calm, although there was a slight flush to his cheeks. 'I think you misunderstood me, Dr Taylor,' he said quietly. 'I didn't say that the remora was a pet, just that we don't know very much about the relationship between it and dolphins. I don't claim to understand everything I see. And I don't regret being a tour guide, as you put it. I simply couldn't afford to do my research if I didn't take paying passengers on board *Honey Bee*, sure, but I happen to think that it's just as important to educate the public about my work as it is to do the research itself.'

Dr Taylor looked uncomfortable now. 'Yes . . . quite . . . public education . . . very important,' he muttered. 'Kind of what I do myself.' He took a deep breath. 'Well, perhaps I spoke out of turn. But I think giving personal names to specimens encourages an unscientific attitude.'

Jody remembered hearing this same argument from Dr Taylor when she had wanted to name the first dolphin she'd befriended, Apollo.

'Well, I find names help my recognition,' Matt said. 'But if it makes you feel better, all the dolphins in my catalogue have an ID number as well.'

Dr Taylor nodded, satisfied with the reply.

Jimmy piped up suddenly: 'I think Lamb is a stupid name for a remora. They don't look anything like lambs!'

'No,' Jody agreed, remembering. 'Actually, it looked more like a tiny shark.'

'Then I'll call him Jaws,' Jimmy announced. He beamed with triumph as the others laughed. 'Baby Jaws!'

3

Honey Bee dropped off the McGraths, Maddie and Dr Taylor at Port Lucaya's marina just after sunset. They quickly found their way to where *Dolphin Dreamer* was docked.

Jody couldn't believe her eyes when she went into the galley to say hi to Mei Lin. There was Brittany, smiling as she chopped up a pile of melons, pineapple, mango and bananas.

'Hi, Jody,' she said cheerily. 'You missed a great afternoon – they've got the coolest marketplace here – and loads of shops selling everything you can think of. It's got to be the best place in the world for shopping! I can't wait to go back tomorrow. How about you? Want to come?'

Jody was still staring at the pile of fruit Brittany was preparing. Brittany hardly ever did any chores. And she'd *never* been this friendly with her before.

Mei Lin looked up from fish fillets she was preparing and smiled warmly. 'Yes, why don't you come with us, Jody?' she suggested.

Jody shook her head. 'Um, thanks, but not tomorrow,' she said apologetically. 'Maybe another time. My folks still have business with Matt, and I really want to see more of those dolphins!'

Brittany wrinkled her nose, but her tone was pleasant enough as she said, 'Well, suit yourself. I'd have thought you would have had enough of being on a boat all day! But guess what,' she went on enthusiastically. 'There's a really great diving school right here in the port. My dad says it's probably the best in the world! We went to check it out this morning, and he's signed me up for a course. And – guess who's going to teach me?' She paused and waited expectantly.

Jody couldn't imagine why Brittany thought she might know. She was still reeling from surprise that Brittany was going to learn how to scuba-dive! 'Is it somebody famous?' she asked.

Brittany laughed. 'No, but I think you've heard of her – she's called Anna, and your parents' friend Matt is her boyfriend! And guess what?' Brittany went on happily. 'She said that if I work hard, I might be able to get my diving certificate within a week!'

'Great!' Jody said. It *was* great that Brittany was going to learn to dive. Maybe she'd come to appreciate the dolphins a bit more while she was underwater! Jody shook her head again. She wasn't used to Brittany talking to her like this!

She reached out to snag a tempting chunk of fresh pineapple and munched it. 'But getting your certificate in one week sounds really fast,' she mused. 'It usually takes much longer – there's an awful lot to learn!' Then she turned to Mei Lin. 'Anything I can do to help?'

'No thanks, Jody, we've got everything under control now,' Mei told her. A delicious smell rose up as the fish fillets began to sizzle in the pan.

July 15 – evening – Port Lucaya.
I just love it here!
Lucaya is a modern, busy resort town, just a few miles from Freeport, which is the main town on Grand Bahama Island. It doesn't look all that different from Florida to

me, but it sure feels different. I haven't seen much of the island yet since we spent most of today out on Honey Bee, *but we saw a little bit of the marina area, on the way back to* Dolphin Dreamer. *Everyone is so friendly. They all seem laid back and happy. It's like even the people who live here are on vacation. Even Brittany seems to have changed her tune. She's going to learn to scuba-dive – and she couldn't wait to tell me all about it, a few minutes ago! I hope her good mood lasts!*

Later, at dinner, Brittany cocked her head and gave Jody a calculating look. 'How long did it take you to get your diving certificate?' she asked.

'I guess I took lessons and did coursework for about three months,' Jody replied. 'But—'

'Well, it won't take *me* that long,' Brittany interrupted. 'I'm a fast learner, all my teachers say so!'

Jody stopped herself from explaining that she'd had to fit her diving sessions into the rest of her life rather than taking an intensive week-long course. She bit her lip and kept quiet, reminding herself that she didn't need to compete with the other girl.

'My mom's going to be amazed when I tell her,' Brittany added.

'Have you heard from her yet?' Jody asked cautiously. She didn't want to dampen Brittany's unusually good mood.

Brittany laughed. 'Well, of course, silly! I knew there'd be an e-mail waiting for me, and there it was! She apologised for being out of touch, and not telling me what was going on, but there was something she just had to do. She's promised to phone real soon and explain everything. She says she's got some wonderful news to tell me!' Brittany concluded with a big grin. 'I'm dying to know what it is!'

'I'm really glad for you,' Jody said warmly. That was true. Life would be better for everyone once Brittany was back where she really wanted to be, she thought.

July 15, continued
At last! A long, juicy e-mail from Lindsay! She hadn't forgotten me at all. Turns out her grandmother wasn't very well, so she went up to Winter Park with her mother to look after her for a few days. No computer in the house, so she couldn't write. But we're back in touch now, and while we're in port we can stay that way. She also reminded me of something I'd forgotten – no e-mail from Devon or Maria because they've gone away to camp!

Next morning, the McGraths and Maddie were up bright and early to join Matt and his tourists on *Honey Bee*.

'No Dr Taylor today?' Matt asked, eyebrows raised, as they came on board.

'I think he's planning to *research* the . . . *non-marine* . . . attractions of the Freeport/Lucaya area today,' Craig explained. He pursed his lips in an imitation of Jefferson Taylor's prissy style. 'But he wanted me to tell you that he's downloaded a copy of your dolphin ID catalogue, and he intends to study it closely.'

'Is he? I'll test him on it, to make sure,' Matt said with a mock scowl.

Jody and her brothers joined Logan and Kim in a prime lookout spot near the front of the boat, each one eager to be the first to spot a dolphin. It was another hot, sunny day, and Jody knew there was nowhere in the world she'd rather be than on a boat gliding through the crystal-clear waters of the Bahamas – unless it was actually *in* the water, with the dolphins!

At first, there was a lot of water traffic to get through. All sorts and sizes of boats were departing from Port Lucaya for a day of sailing, fishing, diving or exploring. But gradually *Honey Bee*'s course took them out to a more peaceful area where they were at last on their own.

'Look,' said Kim suddenly, pointing.

Jody followed the direction of her finger, shading her eyes against the sun. Her heart beat faster as she recognised the unmistakable dorsal fins emerging from the waves. Her father had once pointed out to her that they had the same shape as a thorn on a rose. Then she caught sight of graceful, curved bodies as three dolphins broke surface at the same time before diving down again. Moments later they were swimming alongside the boat.

Logan gave a yell to let everyone else know the dolphins had arrived. Jody leaned over the side to keep watching. As always, the sight of their beautiful, curious faces, wearing what seemed to be a permanent smile, made her smile back. She couldn't help feeling happy whenever there were dolphins around.

Someone on the other side of the boat called out that there were several more dolphins fast approaching.

'Seems like a good place to stop,' said Matt. 'We'll take it slow . . . remember, always take care in the presence of dolphins. A sudden, unexpected stop could be as harmful as too much speed, or a sudden change of direction.'

The dolphins jostled each other in the water, nudging and rubbing against each other as they bobbed up and down, turning their heads to eye the humans curiously.

Jody counted five. She couldn't tell if any of these dolphins had been among those she'd met before, but she was sorry to see no calves in this small group.

And then there were five!

'Do you recognise any of these?' she asked Logan.

The boy shrugged uncertainly. 'I'm not sure . . . Oh yes! That one with a kind of swirly pattern at the back of his head, that's Nebula. But I don't know about the others.'

'Well, these guys are all between six and eleven years old, I'd say,' said Matt, coming up behind Jody.

'Can we go into the water with them?' Jody asked eagerly.

'Not just yet,' Matt replied. 'Remember, easy does it. We'll watch them first, get a feel for their mood. You can talk to them from the boat, I'll play some music, then, if they seem interested, I'll let one or two people get into the water at a time. You build up a better relationship that way.'

Jody nodded, accepting his experience.

'Can I give them a toy to play with?' Logan asked. 'I brought something along.' From his day-pack, he pulled out a bright green frog which squeaked when he squeezed it.

'That looks like a dog-toy,' said Jimmy.

'It is,' Logan agreed. 'But I thought the dolphins might like it.' He looked hopefully at Matt.

Matt laughed and shrugged. 'Sure, why not? They play with things they find in the water all the time.'

Everyone crowded around to watch as Logan leaned over the side with the toy frog in his hand. He squeezed it, making it squeak, and the dolphins responded immediately, whistling and chattering.

'Here you go – it's a present,' Logan called, and tossed the toy overboard.

One of the dolphins – Nebula – shot straight up into the air and nabbed the frog.

Kim clapped her hands. 'Way to go!' she called.

'He won't swallow it, will he?' Jody asked, concerned.

'No, dolphins know what they like to eat, and plastic is not on their menu,' Matt assured her.

Soon the other dolphins were mobbing Nebula, determined to get the frog away from him. He bit down on it, making it squeak, and then dashed away, the others in hot pursuit. Then one of the other dolphins captured the frog, and became 'it'.

Jody and the others watched the game and cheered happily as the dolphins leaped and dived, passing the frog from one to another.

'Uh-oh, here comes trouble.' Matt spoke quietly to Logan's parents, but Jody heard him, and then became aware of the drone of a powerful engine, and the pulsing beat of dance music blasting at top volume.

A boat came speeding past, dangerously close. *Honey Bee* lurched on the wave the passing boat threw up in its wake.

Jody gasped and clutched the side-rail for balance. She gazed down into the water, concerned for the dolphins. But they'd been aware of the approaching speedboat long before she had, and had slipped well below the surface to safety. She could see them gliding along in formation near the bottom.

There were angry exclamations from some of the other passengers. Jody stared out at the speeding launch and read the name in ornate black script on the back: *Stormrider*. She could see four people on board, around nineteen or twenty years old – the college kids Matt had described.

The launch turned in a wide circle and headed back towards *Honey Bee*. The rocking caused by their first pass hadn't even settled down when *Stormrider* ploughed the ocean on the other side, making *Honey Bee* lurch again. Shrieks of taunting laughter carried to them on the breeze.

'They're doing it on purpose!' Jody exclaimed indignantly.

'Try and catch us, little bee,' shouted a girl with

curly red hair as they zoomed past.

They all had bottles in their hands. One of them, a dark, muscular young man, finished his drink and hurled the bottle over the side.

'Hey! Don't litter!' Kim shouted angrily.

'Why don't you get your dolphins to pick it up?' was the reply, causing the passengers on *Stormrider* to shriek again with laughter as they sped away out of sight in a haze of foam and spray.

Gradually the sound of the loud music and the launch's powerful motor died away, as did the huge waves it had left behind.

'Let's hope we've seen the last of them,' sighed Craig.

'Unfortunately, I don't think we're that lucky,' Matt said grimly. 'They've leased that boat for a whole month. Rumour has it that they're here in search of sunken treasure. And even though they seem to spend most of their time zooming around annoying everybody on or in the water, they have diving equipment, and I've even seen them using an underwater metal detector.'

Jody saw the word 'treasure' catch Jimmy and Sean's attention.

'Treasure? What kind of treasure?' demanded

Jimmy, his blue eyes glowing. 'You mean like pirate treasure?'

'Could be,' Matt agreed. 'Hundreds of ships have gone down in these waters, and only a fraction of them have been salvaged. The Bahamas have always been popular with pirates – Captain Kidd, Henry Morgan, Blackbeard, practically every pirate you've ever heard of. If your parents are going to stop off in Nassau, you should visit the Museum of Piracy, and learn all about it.'

'Can we go there, Mom? Dad? Please?' Sean begged, gazing beseechingly at his parents.

Gina smiled. 'Well, we're certainly going to visit Nassau sometime this summer,' she said. 'I'm sure we could manage to fit in a visit to the pirate museum, as a treat for you boys.'

'But what about *real* sunken ships, like the one those guys on *Stormrider* are looking for?' Jimmy asked.

'Well,' said Matt thoughtfully. 'They certainly do exist. I guess you guys are too young to dive yet?'

Jimmy scowled. 'Kids aren't allowed to scuba dive until they're twelve. That means we've got four whole years to wait. I can't wait that long to find treasure!' He sounded outraged.

Jody tried not to laugh.

'Well, maybe you'll get lucky,' Matt said kindly. 'This part of the world is full of stories of people who found gold or jewels while they were beachcombing, or snorkelling, or just floating along in an inner-tube, looking into the shallows.'

'They just sound like stories to attract more tourists,' said Gina with an indulgent smile.

'No, the stories are true,' Matt declared. 'I know, because it happened to my friend Ismay Collins! She came to Grand Bahama Island on vacation, found some pieces of eight on a deserted beach, and it changed her whole life!'

'What are pieces of eight?' Logan asked with a puzzled frown.

'Pirate coins,' Jimmy told him.

'Actually, they're coins made from one ounce of pure silver, minted by the Spanish in the New World from the 1530s onward,' Maddie put in.

They all looked at her in surprise. 'Are you a treasure-hunter, too?' asked Matt.

Maddie shook her head, smiling. 'No, but history is a hobby of mine. With the boys so interested in pirates, I've been reading up on the subject. Now I'm puzzled: how did finding a few silver coins change your friend's life? Pieces of eight aren't *that* valuable!'

'The find didn't make her rich,' Matt agreed, nodding. 'But it gave her the itch to find more. She teamed up with her brother, Alex, to buy a boat, and they come out here every summer to look for the lost pirate shipwreck. It's all legal and above-board. They call themselves The New Treasure Seekers, and they've got a salvage permit from the government, but so far, alas, they haven't found another bit of treasure.' He stopped and looked around at his audience.

Jody realised that everyone on board *Honey Bee* had gathered around Matt to listen to him.

'And . . . believe it or not, I haven't gotten quite as far off the subject of dolphins as you might think,' he told them now. 'There's a very famous wreck called the *Maravilla*, a Spanish galleon which sank in the Bahama Channel on New Year's Day of 1656, while carrying a load of treasure back to Spain. Divers at the time managed to recover some of it, but the rest was thought to be lost forever . . . Until, in the early 1970s, a man found an old document in a Spanish library. It was an eyewitness account of the wreck. From it, he figured out exactly where the ship must have gone down, and started diving in the area until he found it. Since then, many thousands – possibly millions! – of dollars worth of treasure – gold, silver, jewels, even a complete elephant tusk – has been found. Divers are still hunting for more.'

'Is there anything left?' Maddie asked curiously.

Matt nodded. 'There's a record of everything the ship was carrying, and lots of it has never been found. Like, a life-sized, solid gold statue of the Madonna, for example!'

Craig let out a low whistle. 'How does something that big get hidden?' he wondered.

'The same way whole ships are lost,' Matt told him. 'It's buried somewhere under the sand. A storm comes along, high winds, water-spouts, whirlpools – you can't believe how fierce they are if you've never experienced a tropical storm! Of course, the damage when they move inland is awful. We all know about that. But the storms also tear up the seabed, places most people never see. All that soft sand under the water is stirred around like somebody took a gigantic spoon to it. Afterwards, nothing is the same. Stuff lying down there gets broken up, thrown around, and buried ten, twenty, thirty metres deep.'

Jody tried to imagine it. But she found herself distracted by something Matt had said earlier. 'But what does all this have to do with dolphins?' she asked.

Matt laughed. 'Thanks for bringing me back to my point, Jody! I'm an awful rambler when I get going. OK – except for the famous dolphins of Monkey Mia in Australia, the spotted dolphins of Little Bahama Bank are among the friendliest in the world!'

He paused, then went on. 'In my opinion, it's the divers we have to thank. For years, people have been diving into the wreck, and the dolphins have been watching them. Because divers have their own work to do, they don't have the usual grabby response when dolphins come near. They just get on with their work. They respect the dolphins, and the dolphins respect them.' He looked around at everyone. 'When you all go away from here, I want you to remember that these are special dolphins.'

'They sure are!' Logan put in enthusiastically, and there was a general chorus of agreement.

Matt put up a hand for silence. 'I mean, if you happen to encounter wild dolphins somewhere else in the world, or even somewhere else in the Caribbean, don't go expecting that they'll be as interested in you and as friendly as the dolphins here. Maybe they will be, but chances are that if you get into the water hoping to swim with them, any other dolphins would be outta there!'

Gina raised her hand like someone in a class. Matt pointed at her. 'Here's another dolphin expert to confirm what I say!'

'It's true, I've encountered a lot of dolphins, and I've been surprised by how especially friendly your lot are,' she told him. 'I thought it must be because they were used to you, and trusted you.'

'I wish I could claim all the credit,' Matt replied. 'But when I first arrived, the dolphins welcomed me with, er, open fins, as it were. They were already used to people, and had a good impression of us, thanks to the divers working on shipwrecks in the area. Especially, the *Maravilla*.'

He had been looking very serious as he spoke, but now he relaxed and a smile lit up his face. 'End of lecture. I hope you understood the lesson? Now, let's get back to looking for dolphins!'

4

July 19 – evening.

Met some bottlenose dolphins today. Five of them came up to Honey Bee with ten Atlantic spotted dolphins. Then people started getting into the water. The spotted dolphins were as friendly as always, but the bottlenose kept their distance, and swam away after a few minutes.

It made me think about my first dolphin friend, Apollo. I wonder how he is. Does he ever think of me? Will we meet again when we get back to Florida – and will he remember me? Matt says dolphins have excellent memories, and seem to be able to remember people they have met years before. I hope so.

Brittany is real busy learning to dive – and that has

definitely *been a good influence on her! I don't think she is finding it quite as easy as she expected, and maybe that has given her a little more respect for me? Anyway, she's a lot nicer, and sharing a cabin with her isn't such a hardship any more – even though I'd still swap her for Lindsay in a hot second!*

'Hey, Jody? What do you think of this lipstick?' Startled, Jody looked up from her diary to discover Brittany pouting dark red lips at her.

'Oh, I don't know,' she said cautiously. 'What's the point?'

'The point is to look more grown up,' Brittany explained, examining herself in a small mirror.

'Will your dad let you wear it?' Jody asked.

Brittany hunched her shoulders, sighed, and began to wipe her lips with a tissue. 'Probably not, the old dinosaur. Some of his ideas are positively prehistoric!' She rolled her eyes.

Jody liked Harry too much to take sides against him. 'Does your mom let you wear make-up?' she asked.

Brittany wriggled uncomfortably. 'Well . . . I think she would . . . at least, on special occasions . . . it hasn't really come up,' she confessed. Then she added quickly, 'She did give me this lipstick, though. It's one of her old ones.' She brightened. 'Did I tell you she sent me another e-mail? She's going to call next week for sure!'

'That's great,' Jody said warmly. She closed her diary and stowed it away. 'Have you told her about learning to dive?'

'No, I'm saving that for when she calls. Hopefully, I'll have my Open Water Certificate by then! That'll *really* surprise her!'

There was a knock at the cabin door, and then Gina looked in, smiling. 'Hi, girls. Come on out – we've got visitors.'

Harry and Craig were in the saloon with Matt and Anna – a short, strong-looking young woman with curly black hair and a calm, self-confident manner.

Anna shook Jody firmly by the hand and gave Brittany a brief hug. 'How's my star pupil?' she asked.

Jody was surprised to see Brittany blush and duck her head shyly. 'I'm not really . . .' she muttered.

'Sure you are!' Anna declared. 'You went through the theory like it was a bag of candy! Never known anybody learn so fast. You've got it all up here.' She tapped her head. 'Now we've got to bring it out there.' She stretched out her arms as if to embrace the world.

'You need more self-confidence. Say "I'm a star" – go on, say it!'

Brittany giggled and rolled her eyes. 'I'm a star,' she muttered self-consciously.

Jody felt very glad nobody was putting her on the spot like that. Anna seemed nice, but she was rather theatrical!

'And you're ready to dive in,' Anna announced. 'That's what I've come about.' She looked at Craig and Gina. 'Matt tells me you're not going out on *Honey Bee* tomorrow, but you're going on your own boat to look for dolphins?'

'We want to do some underwater filming,' Gina explained. 'Matt's given Harry the coordinates for a spot where he's pretty sure we'll find some dolphins.'

'Yes, he told me,' Anna replied. 'Of course, there's never any guarantee with dolphins, but it's a perfect spot for diving and filming,' she went on. 'Clear water, great visibility, and well under ten metres deep.'

'Sounds ideal,' Gina said, smiling.

'Ideal for an inexperienced diver, too,' Anna said. 'If you agree, Brittany and I could come along for her first experience of diving from a boat.'

'Sure, that would be fine,' Gina agreed.

Jody heard Brittany gasp. She looked and saw that

Brittany had gone pale and wide-eyed.

'I can't – I need more practice,' Brittany said nervously. 'I'm not ready for deep diving yet!'

'Of course you need practice,' said Anna. 'Practice is what you will get! It's not deep diving – the water will be very shallow. I will be there beside you always, don't worry about that, honey.'

'But – I don't think – I'm not really—'

'If you're not happy about it, love, then of course you don't have to go,' Harry put in, sounding concerned.

Anna gave a little frown and shook her head at him before turning her attention back to Brittany. 'It's the next step,' she said firmly. 'You can't learn any more from swimming-pool practice. If you don't want to take the next step, the lessons stop here. Pity, because you've been doing so well. Do you want to go on with your lessons, and learn to dive, or are you going to give up now?'

There was a silence. Jody didn't know where to look. She saw Harry looking, uncomfortably, down at his shoes. She felt sorry for Brittany, and also surprised. Brittany had sounded so enthusiastic, she could hardly believe she'd been hiding fear behind her confident words.

Finally Brittany spoke. Her voice sounded small but determined. 'I'll do it.'

'Of course you will, sweetheart, of course you will!' Anna boomed cheerily, smiling broadly.

Jody sighed with relief.

It was another beautiful day. The brilliantly blue water sparkled in the sun, and *Dolphin Dreamer* raced smoothly along under full sail. Jody stood by herself on the forward deck, leaning against the side and scanning the waves for any sign of dolphins. She thought how peaceful it was to be without the twins, for a change. Sean and Jimmy had gone out on *Honey Bee* that morning. It was their last chance to see Logan, who would be flying home with his parents the next day.

Soon she heard Harry call, 'Prepare to come about!' and she scrambled to get out of the way as Cam and her father began pulling on lines and taking in the sails to slow the boat's progress.

She joined Harry at the helm. 'Is this really the place Matt suggested?' she asked, feeling a little worried. 'I haven't seen any dolphins at all.'

Harry Pierce screwed his bearded face into a mock scowl. 'Are you questioning my ability to navigate, young lady?' he said in his gruff, English accent.

'You'd better not doubt the captain,' Cam laughed as he fastened down the mainsail. '*Dolphin Dreamer* has all the most up-to-date navigational aids, but if he had to Harry could find his way by dead reckoning, at night, in a thunderstorm!'

'I just hope I never have to prove it,' said Harry, his mouth twisting wryly.

Jody looked out at the empty expanse of bright blue water. 'How can Matt know they'll be here?' she wondered aloud.

Gina came up and put a hand on her shoulder. 'I'm sure they'll turn up,' she said. 'Matt knows what he's talking about. He's been keeping track of the local dolphins for a long time. Over the years he's managed to build up a really good picture – a sort of "dolphin map" of the Little Bahama Bank, showing changes over the course of the year.'

'That's why he's able to provide such a great tour service,' Craig said. 'He can pretty much guarantee dolphin sightings every day he goes out. But it has much greater implications. The sort of map Matt has drawn up could help people avoid dolphins as well as find them. That could cut way down on the deaths of dolphins caused by fishing or any sort of undersea industry, like oil exploration.'

Dr Taylor had been sitting in the shade, reading a book. He looked up at Craig's last words. 'That's very interesting,' he said. 'But how accurate is this map? If we don't see any dolphins today, we'll have to wonder!'

'Oh, I don't think there's any worry about that,' said Craig softly. He was gazing out to sea, a big smile on his face.

Jody turned to follow her father's gaze and thrilled to the sight of about a dozen Atlantic spotted dolphins swimming directly towards the boat.

'Come on,' said Gina urgently. 'Let's get a move on before they get bored and leave!'

A short time later Jody rejoined her parents, Anna and Brittany to discuss their dive plan and check all the equipment.

Brittany was looking pale and nervous, chewing her lip. Anna patted her arm. 'Let's run through those hand-signals, make sure you remember them all. How many are there?'

'Nine,' said Brittany in a small voice. 'This means, *Are you OK?* or, *I'm OK*.' She demonstrated the sign with her hand at head-level, finger and thumb joined to make a circle, the other three straight. She went through the rest of the basic signals every diver must know, seeming to gain confidence as she proved she could communicate with her dive-partner and the others underwater.

Meanwhile, Jody's father was double-checking her equipment. He would be her dive-partner, although he would also be alert for any signals from Gina.

'This air-tank is awfully heavy,' Brittany complained after Anna had helped her put it on her back. 'I'll be exhausted in about five minutes!' She made the fingers-spread *out of breath* sign that divers use when they need to rest and recover.

Anna chuckled. 'Maybe, if you were running around on land. Remember, it'll feel a lot lighter in the water! OK, partner, I think we're ready to dive!'

Craig McGrath was the first to 'giant-stride' into the water, followed soon after by Jody. Then came Brittany, then Anna, and finally Gina. Cam handed down the video camera to Gina. They all swapped *OK* signals after they were submerged, and then Anna pointed out the direction she and Brittany would take.

As always, Jody was thrilled to be in the undersea world. She loved having the same view of things as a dolphin. Here, in the shallows of Little Bahama Bank, where the water was so clear, and the brilliant white sand reflected back so much light, was more magical than anywhere else she'd ever been.

She saw a brightly coloured parrot fish hovering in the water to her right. On her left, a small school of yellow-and-blue angelfish were passing, indifferent to her presence. Something nudged her arm and she turned her head. To her astonishment and delight she saw the familiar, perpetual smile and warm round eye of a curious dolphin.

Jody knew immediately that it was a calf from its smaller size and lack of spots, so she looked around for the mother. As soon as she turned her head she saw three adult dolphins swimming in close formation. They circled her, swimming smoothly around until the calf joined the group.

Jody saw that one of the adults had a remora clinging to her side, and knew that this was Mary with Baby Jaws, and that the calf, now nuzzling affectionately against Mary, was certainly Skipper. She felt happy to meet them again, and, as she looked more carefully at the other two adults, thought she recognised them as Cressy and Nebula.

Nebula had a long strand of seaweed draped over his tail. He swam past Mary and Skipper, the long green fronds waving gently in the water. Mary suddenly flipped onto her side and shot away. Jody blinked in surprise. Now the seaweed was hanging from Mary's tail!

Skipper raced after his mother. He tried to grab at the seaweed with his mouth, but Mary kept it out of his reach. Then he swam under her. Mary dipped her tail and the strand of seaweed floated for a moment before Skipper caught it on his tail and swam directly towards Jody.

Skipper having fun with seaweed.

Jody was thrilled as she realised Skipper was inviting her to play. She finned closer to him and stretched out her arms to take the seaweed. But Skipper kept it out of her reach; Jody guessed it was cheating to use either mouth or arms in the seaweed game. But she did think she was a bit handicapped in not having a tail like the other players!

Still, she would do her best. She kicked herself closer to Skipper and tried to hook the seaweed with one of her fins. But it was harder than it looked, especially since Skipper wouldn't stay still. In fact, all of the dolphins were constantly in motion, swimming over and under and around each other.

After three or four failures, Jody was feeling awfully clumsy. She was getting ready to try again when she realised that the seaweed was no longer hanging from Skipper's tail. Somehow, Mary had it again. She swam past Jody . . . and Jody, startled, felt the soft fronds of the weed land gently across her ankles. She'd barely realised it was there before Nebula, swimming past her on her other side, flicked his tail and claimed it back.

Whatever the rules were in this game, Jody realised she couldn't compete. But that didn't matter. She had a wonderful warm feeling inside from knowing the dolphins accepted her as a friend. She was happy just to watch them play, and to admire their grace and beauty.

Her undersea experience seemed to have transformed Brittany. Back on deck, she was bubbling over with emotion. 'Gosh, it's so gorgeous down there! It's wonderful! I wish we could have stayed longer, though. I was so nervous at first, but then, just when I felt like I was starting to get the hang of it, we had to come up!' Then her excitement gave way to anxiety. 'Did I do OK?' she appealed to Anna, who smiled at her warmly.

'You were fine,' Anna assured her. 'There are some things you need to work on. We'll talk about those when you fill in your logbook. Now, let's get this equipment safely stored away.'

Jody felt pleased for Brittany as she hurried away to get changed and jot a few notes in her own logbook. She would fill in more details later, she decided. Right now, she wanted to watch the dolphins while they were still close by.

As she leaned over the side, Jody saw that quite a crowd had gathered, clicking and whistling to each other as they swam under and around *Dolphin*

Dreamer. She grinned happily as she counted fifteen dolphins. A few she recognised straight away – Mary and Skipper, of course, and Nebula, Debby and Dobbin – the others she couldn't be sure of so quickly. She wondered if *Honey Bee* was having as much luck, wherever she was today. This was obviously *the* best place for dolphin-spotting!

Somewhere in the distance was a low, droning sound, gradually getting louder. Jody recognised it as the motor of an approaching boat.

When she turned to look she saw that the boat was *Stormrider*. And it was heading straight for them.

5

Stormrider came roaring by, churning the water into a foaming wake. Jody was not surprised when the dolphins scattered. But then she saw that while most of the dolphins were swimming rapidly away, four or five were now heading directly towards the motor launch. And one of them was Skipper.

'No!' she cried out, clutching the side-rail and staring in horror. In her mind was what Matt had told her about dolphins being badly hurt by propellors.

Dolphins liked to play in the wake of fast-moving boats, she knew. But she was afraid that this time their playfulness and curiosity would get them into trouble.

She held her breath. Mary and Nebula were racing after Skipper. They closed in on the young dolphin from both sides and firmly steered him away to safety.

Jody sighed with relief. But the other dolphins continued on their course. She watched as three adult dolphins began to leap about in the spray and 'surf' the wave left in *Stormrider*'s wake.

The *Stormrider* crew must have noticed this activity, because they began to clap and cheer. They were very close now, and the sound carried clearly. Then, with a suddenness which could have been dangerous for the dolphins who followed them, the motor cut out, and the launch rocked and slowed to a halt just behind *Dolphin Dreamer*.

Jody saw her parents exchange puzzled looks with Harry and Cam.

'I'll see what they want,' said Harry. 'Ahoy, *Stormrider*!' he called.

'What's going on?' Brittany came up beside Jody. She stared over at the other boat, and her expression brightened with interest. 'Ooh, those guys are cute,' she said admiringly. 'That boat looks expensive, too!'

Jody shot a withering glance at Brittany, but the

other girl was too fascinated with the *Stormrider* crew to notice her disapproval.

There were four people on board the launch, all standing and staring at *Dolphin Dreamer* in a most unfriendly way. They didn't respond to Harry's greeting.

A blonde girl in a bright pink swimsuit said, 'Marcus, tell them to shove off!' Whether or not she meant to be overheard, her voice was loud and carried clearly.

The dark, muscular young man shrugged and muttered something.

The blonde frowned angrily and looked at the other boy. 'Jay, can't you do something?'

'Yeah,' said Jay. He spoke so loudly Jody thought it had to be deliberate. 'I am going to party! Heather, put on some music. Loud as it'll go!'

The red-haired girl nodded enthusiastically and scrambled into the cabin. Moments later, loud, pounding music began to pulse out into the peaceful air.

Jody saw Harry wince as, next to her, Brittany was moving her body in time to the beat.

Jay and Marcus put their heads together for a moment, and then Marcus yelled, 'Bring me beer! Lots of beer!'

Jay gave an ear-splitting yell – 'Yeee-haaaa!' – grabbed the blonde girl and started a clumsy dance.

'We might as well leave,' said Gina, sighing.

'Yeah, that's what they want us to do,' Craig said. He nodded at Harry to pull up the anchor. His blue eyes narrowed thoughtfully. He spoke very quietly. 'Funny, if they didn't want company, why'd they come here?'

Gina's eyes widened. 'You mean, they came to chase us off?'

Jody frowned, and stared across at the launch. They were all making a lot of noise, whooping and yelling, as if they were having a great time, but something about it didn't ring true. Then she noticed the diving equipment. There were four air-tanks standing neatly in a row. The party was just a pretence. They had come here to dive, and, for some reason, they didn't want anyone to know . . .

July 20 – bedtime.
They're looking for treasure! And they seem to think it's in that area. But we didn't see any sign of a shipwreck, so they're wrong. Or are they? It could be hiding somewhere close by . . . Now their dolphin-chasing behaviour makes a weird kind of sense . . . that's one of

Matt's favourite spots to take Honey Bee. *Chasing the dolphins away chases* him *away, so there's no witnesses if they find anything. Matt told us that all finds in the Bahamas have to be reported, and shared with the government (they take twenty-five per cent). I bet these guys are planning to keep it all for themselves.*

Brittany is so silly sometimes. She has decided that the one called Jay looks just like her favourite TV star, and thinks that the girls are cool because they were wearing expensive swimsuits and designer sunglasses . . . She doesn't care that the things they do could hurt dolphins; she says I'm the one who is silly – about dolphins! I am totally fed up with her . . .

'There they are!' Brittany's whisper buzzed in Jody's ear as they entered the air-conditioned coffee-shop.

'What? Who?' Jody frowned, puzzled. Several days had passed since their encounter with *Stormrider*, and it was far from her mind. She'd just spent an exhausting hour with her brothers at the adventure playground near the marina, and was looking forward to sitting down and having a cool drink before heading back to *Dolphin Dreamer*.

'Shh! Pretend you haven't noticed them!' Brittany giggled behind her hand and darted her eyes in the direction she wanted Jody to look.

Jody's heart sank as she recognised the four college kids who'd chartered *Stormrider*. They were sitting around a table crowded with coffee-cups and pieces of paper, including a big navigational chart.

Marcus was holding something that looked like an old-fashioned parchment and jabbing his finger at the chart as he argued with the others.

Jody didn't want to sit anywhere near them. Unfortunately, the twins had already dashed ahead and settled into a booth directly opposite the *Stormrider* party, so she had no choice.

Brittany sat up very straight and licked her lips. She toyed with her hair. Jody even saw her check her appearance using the back of a spoon as a mirror!

When the waitress came, Jody, who had been given the money by her father, ordered ice cream sundaes all around, and Cokes for herself and the boys. She looked at Brittany inquiringly.

'I'd like a coffee with mine,' Brittany said loudly.

Jody raised her eyebrows, surprised. 'You don't usually drink coffee!'

'Yes I do. I love coffee,' Brittany declared.

Jody shrugged and didn't argue. She guessed Brittany was trying to seem grown-up in the hope of attracting the college kids' attention. But they were much too preoccupied with their own discussion to notice anyone else. Jody didn't want to eavesdrop, but, as the argument grew louder, she couldn't help but overhear.

'It's right here,' Marcus was saying, jabbing a spoon at the chart. 'We *know* that. This spot absolutely fits the description to a "T". It's lying buried under the sand. I say we rent a bigger boat and a prop-wash and blow that baby out!'

'It could be anywhere within a twenty-mile radius. No sense wasting more money till we've narrowed it down,' Jay objected. 'We've already got the metal-detector, so let's use it some more. Another week of diving, maybe less – we're bound to get lucky!'

'You talk like we've got forever,' the blonde girl said, frowning. 'We've got to go home in less than two weeks. If we don't find something soon . . .'

'Calm down, Ally,' said the red-haired girl, patting her hand. 'Why don't we take a vote?'

'OK,' said Marcus. 'I vote we rent a bigger boat and prop-wash tomorrow.'

Jay frowned. 'Easy for you to say. Don't forget who's paying for this . . .'

'Yeah, rich boy, and don't forget who did all the

research into the sinking of the *Elvira* and found the eye-witness accounts, and the map! We wouldn't have got very far without this!' Marcus rattled his parchment in Jay's face.

Sean and Jimmy looked at each other, their eyes big and round. Before Jody or Brittany could even try to stop them, both boys had scrambled out of the booth and were leaning across the next table, struggling with each other to be the first to get a good look at it.

'Is that a treasure map?' Jimmy demanded.

'It looks like a real pirate's map!' Sean crowed excitedly. 'Please, can we see it? Please, we know lots and lots of stuff about pirates.'

'We could help you!' Jimmy added.

Marcus held the piece of parchment high out of the boys' reach.

'Now look what you've done,' Jay snarled, glaring furiously at Marcus. 'Telling the whole world . . . if you'd keep your big mouth shut—' He snatched the ancient map out of his friend's hand and stashed it in a briefcase lying open on a chair beside him. Ally, meanwhile, was busily rolling up the navigational chart.

'Aw, they're just kids,' Marcus said.

'So are we,' said Ally. 'Just big kids.' She smiled broadly at Sean and Jimmy. 'It's just pretend, you know. Just a little game we're playing, to make our vacation more fun.'

Jody could see her brothers weren't fooled.

'Didn't look like a pretend map to me,' said Sean, frowning.

Jimmy attempted his own sly approach: 'We've made up treasure maps, too. You show us yours, and we'll show you ours, OK?'

'No deal,' said Jay firmly. 'But I'll tell you what. You be nice to us, and we'll be nice to you. All you have to do is keep your mouths shut, don't tell anyone what you've heard today, and then, if we *do* happen to find any treasure, we just might share it with you. To prove it, I'll give you a little advance on that treasure, right now.' He dug into his pocket and pulled out a handful of crumpled bills.

Jody was furious. But she didn't have to say a word. At the sight of the money, Sean and Jimmy backed away, shaking their heads.

'Aw, come on, don't be like that – what's wrong, isn't it enough?' Jay wheedled.

'We aren't allowed to take money from strangers,' Jimmy said firmly.

What's Brittany playing at?

'You're right, you shouldn't even be talking to us,' said Ally swiftly. 'Better not tell your parents – they might get mad! We'll just pretend this whole thing never happened, OK?'

'Fine with me,' Jody said coldly, and steered her younger brothers back to their table.

'Don't worry,' she heard Brittany say. 'We won't tell anybody. I figure if somebody is smart enough to figure out where to find a treasure, then they ought to be allowed to keep it.'

'You sound like a smart kid,' said Jay.

Then the waitress arrived with their order, and the next few moments were taken up with exclamations from the boys about the size of the sundaes, before settling down to the serious business of eating.

Brittany strolled over to pick up her coffee and ice cream. 'Ally invited me to go and sit with them,' she said, smirking proudly on her return. 'Guess what? Heather's cousins live in West Palm Beach. I bet we even know some of the same people!'

Jody watched her go, feeling uneasy. She didn't like the *Stormrider* crew, and she didn't like the idea of Brittany getting involved with them. But she couldn't think of any way to stop her from doing as she liked.

6

Matt and Anna joined them on board *Dolphin Dreamer* for dinner that evening. Mei Lin had decided to try her hand at some local Bahamian specialties. She served up conch salad as a starter, followed by some sort of local fish cooked in a spicy tomato sauce, accompanied by huge helpings of golden brown peas and rice. For dessert there was fresh fruit salad.

'Hey, Matt,' said Sean, pushing aside his bowl after picking out the banana, which was the one fruit on offer that he was willing to eat, 'you were right about those guys on *Stormrider*. They *are* looking for sunken treasure. They've even got a map! Hey, do you think we could get there ahead of them and find the treasure first?'

'You little rat!' Brittany exclaimed, frowning fiercely. 'You weren't supposed to tell anybody!'

'We never said we wouldn't,' Jimmy answered for his brother.

'You're the only one who said you wouldn't tell,' Jody reminded Brittany. 'And I don't see why we shouldn't. They don't have any special right to that treasure.'

'Well, I think they do. They're the ones who did the research and found the map. And they've paid for the boat and diving equipment and everything. And I like them,' Brittany finished, her chin high.

Jody shrugged. She didn't trust that group. And she thought Brittany only wanted to make herself seem more grown-up by pretending she had older friends.

'Unless you can sketch the map from memory, I'd say there's no chance of us finding this mysterious wreck,' Matt said to Sean.

Sean looked disappointed. He shook his head. 'I hardly saw the map,' he confessed. 'But I know the name of the ship. It's called *Elvira*.'

'*Elvira!*' exclaimed Anna. She looked at Matt. 'That's

the name of the shipwreck Alex and Ismay are looking for!'

'You're sure of the name?' Matt asked Sean. Both twins nodded vigorously.

'It must be the same ship,' Matt said, exchanging a glance with Anna. 'So they've found a map. Well, well . . .' He shook his head. 'My friends spend three summers searching for the wreck without any luck, and then these guys come along with a map! It probably won't do them much good, though. They don't seem to be very organised about their search. I think they're time-wasters, really. Amateurs. Even knowing the general area where a ship went down doesn't mean you'll be able to pinpoint the spot where it is now. There've been centuries of storms to smash it to bits and bury those pieces deep under the sand.'

'But didn't you say your friends found some coins that came from it?' Jody asked.

Matt nodded. 'They found them washed up on a beach right after a big storm. Possibly some part of the ship was uncovered then. Unfortunately, it was hurricane season, and there were even bigger storms to come. By the time Alex and Ismay had a chance to start diving, *Elvira* must have been completely buried again.'

'Coffee, anyone?' asked Mei Lin as she began to clear away the plates with Cam's help.

Brittany frowned at Matt in a puzzled way. 'Don't your friends know about using a prop-wash?' she asked. 'That's what *my* friends are going to use. Ally and Heather explained it to me. The prop-wash fits over the boat's propeller and sticks down deep in the water. They anchor the boat so it can't move, and they run the engine, and the prop-wash creates like a whirlpool which blows away the sand and uncovers the wreck.'

'Yes, if the wreck is there,' Matt agreed. 'Otherwise, all you end up with is a nice, empty hollow in the sand! There's an awful lot of ocean floor to just dig at random! But if your friends have a good map, they may get lucky.'

'Your own friends must have some idea where the wreck of the *Elvira* is meant to be,' said Craig, leaning across the table, his eyes bright with interest. 'Did they ever tell you where they thought it was?'

Matt looked back at his old friend and laughed as he shook his head. 'Don't tell me the treasure-hunting bug has bitten you, too!'

'No, no,' Craig protested, unconvincingly. 'I just thought it might be interesting for the kids . . .' His voice trailed off, and he rubbed his face, looking a little embarrassed.

'As a matter of fact,' said Matt slowly, 'you've been there. It's the very place where you got that great underwater footage of the dolphins playing the seaweed game with Jody.'

'You mean where I had my first open-sea dive?' Brittany asked, sounding startled. 'I never saw anything that looked like a shipwreck!'

'Neither did I,' said Gina. 'But it's a great spot for filming – shallow, great visibility, and popular with dolphins. In fact, I really would like to go back, only . . .'

Jody thought she knew what her mother was thinking, and finished her sentence for her: 'If *Stormrider* is there they'll scare off the dolphins. And if they think that's where the wreck is, they're bound to be there every day.' She exchanged a resigned look with her mother.

Craig sighed, and took a sip of coffee. 'No point in looking for trouble,' he agreed. 'We'll find another spot for filming . . . or maybe just spend tomorrow analysing some more of Matt's files. You've collected enough raw data to keep half a dozen graduate students busy for ten years!'

Matt grinned. 'It's to give you something to do during those long winter nights at sea,' he said. 'I don't think you should spend your time on it while you're here. Get in as much underwater filming as you can before the weather turns. After all, there's plenty of other places you could try . . .'

Brittany spoke up unexpectedly. '*Stormrider* won't be there tomorrow,' she said. 'They're taking a day off from treasure-hunting. The boys are going deep-sea fishing. Ally and Heather think fishing is boring, so they're going shopping in Freeport.' She turned to her father, who had said almost nothing throughout the meal, and gazed at him appealingly. 'They said I could go with them. May I, Daddy? Please?'

'I need to meet these girls, first, and have a chat with them,' Harry said cautiously.

Brittany beamed confidently. 'I thought you might say that! They told me they'd be in the coffee-shop tomorrow morning for breakfast. You could go and meet them then.'

Harry must have decided that Ally and Heather were trustworthy, Jody thought, because when *Dolphin Dreamer* cast off the next day, it was without Brittany.

But Mei Lin also stayed behind – she would travel in to Freeport with the three girls, do her own shopping, and then meet up with Brittany later in the day.

Jody leaned against the rail and watched the sails fill with wind as she inhaled the warm salt air. The sun shone down out of a clear blue sky as it had every day they had been here. Gazing out at the gentle waves on the turquoise water she found it hard to believe that there could be hundreds of shipwrecks lying down below.

Behind her, she could hear Cam talking to the twins: 'Yeah, I've been treasure-hunting. Never found anything, though. But I always used to hope. See, my dad found seven gold coins on the beach when he was a little boy, so I was always on the look-out.'

'Was it pirate treasure?' Jimmy asked. Both boys were listening with breathless attention.

'No, nothing to do with pirates. These were Spanish coins from about 1700, and my dad was pretty sure where they came from. Back in 1715, a convoy of twelve ships were carrying treasure from the Spanish colony in Cuba, back home to Spain. A hurricane struck as they were sailing up the Straits of Florida at the end of July, and . . .' he slapped his hands together. 'Four ships were sunk.'

It was nearly the end of July now, Jody thought. She turned away from the calm sea to ask Cam, 'Isn't the end of July early for a hurricane?'

Cam nodded. 'Hurricane season's really not supposed to start before the end of August,' he agreed. 'But you can get a big storm any time. Out here, they can boil up fast and fierce. And back in the old days, sailors didn't have the benefit of satellites, and weather tracking stations, or radio to warn them to get in to shelter.'

Although he could obviously hear this discussion from his place at the helm, Harry Pierce was keeping very quiet.

Jody noticed a slight frown on the man's bearded, weather-beaten face. She wondered if he was worried about Brittany. Hoping to distract him, Jody asked, 'Harry, have *you* ever seen a shipwreck?'

'Yes, I'm sorry to say I have,' he answered in a low voice. 'And it's not something I'd like to see again.' Then he gave himself a little shake. 'But that's not what you meant, is it? I'm sorry – I can't get excited about sunken treasure. It feels unlucky to me. I guess I'm just a superstitious old sailor! But when I hear about a shipwreck, even if it happened hundreds of years ago, I can't help imagining the people who were on board, and what it must have been like for them.'

Jody felt as if a game of pretend had suddenly turned serious. She didn't know what to say. She was glad when a sudden cry from her mother, on the foredeck, grabbed their attention:

'Dolphins approaching to starboard!'

Jody forgot all about pirates, treasure, sunken ships and everything else as she raced to the side and looked. A group of about a dozen Atlantic spotted dolphins were swimming rapidly towards them. Occasionally, one at a time, they would leap through the air, seemingly for the sheer joy of it. But even when they were swimming entirely beneath the water she could see them clearly.

Soon, they had reached *Dolphin Dreamer* and began to compete with each other to ride the wave produced as the sailboat cut through the water. Now they were near enough to be identified, especially as they jumped up, playfully knocking each other aside.

Jody stretched out her hand, and one of the leaping dolphins just brushed it with the rounded top of its head. She wasn't quite sure, but she thought it was Nebula.

She watched carefully, trying to recognise some of

the dolphins she had met before. Was that Cressy? And Mystic and Oberon? Scar-fin's damaged dorsal fin was unmistakable. When she'd spotted him she was pretty sure she was right about the others. She was sorry not to see the ones who had become her favourites – Mary, with her 'pet' remora, and her calf Skipper. All of the dolphins now playing alongside *Dolphin Dreamer* were adults; there weren't any babies in this group.

Jody was careful to keep out of the way as Cam and her father scrambled about pulling on lines and taking in the sails to slow the boat's progress. She was worried at first that the dolphins would abandon them once the boat was no longer moving, but these dolphins were used to visitors. They knew what to expect, and from the way they hung about, it seemed they were as eager to play with humans as Jody and her family were to swim with them.

'We're ready! Can we go swimming now, please?' Sean and Jimmy's voices chimed together. Jody stared at her twin brothers in disbelief. They must have raced below and changed into their swimsuits in literally half a minute, she thought.

'You boys know you can't go in on your own,' Gina said. 'Your dad, Jody and I are going diving, so–'

'I could go in too and keep an eye on them,' Cam volunteered.

'Oh, Cam, that's very kind of you,' Gina replied with a warm smile. 'Thank you. OK,' she went on, as Sean and Jimmy began to cheer, 'you'll get your swim, but remember to do exactly as Cam tells you.'

'And try not to act like you outnumber me,' Cam advised them sternly. 'Even though you do.'

'Maybe I could even things out by joining your team,' Maddie suggested. She looked at Gina and Craig. 'If you don't need me for anything, that is.'

'I was only going to ask you to keep an eye on the tape-recorder,' Gina said. 'But maybe Dr Taylor would do that?'

At the sound of his name the portly scientist, who had been resting in the shade of an oversized straw hat, suddenly jerked upright, as if startled awake. 'Er, what was that?' he asked.

Gina explained that they would be using the hydrophone – an underwater microphone – to record sounds made by the dolphins, and needed someone on board to monitor it and change the tape if necessary.

'No trouble at all – only too happy to contribute,' he exclaimed. 'And if there's anything else – you will let me know if there are any other little jobs that need doing?'

He sounded grateful to have something to do, Jody thought – as if Gina was doing him a favour instead of the other way round. For the first time it occurred to her that maybe he wasn't exactly thrilled about being a sort of tag-along, instead of a vital member of the Dolphin Universe team.

It was not much longer before Jody and her parents were kitted up and in the water. As she descended, Jody was aware of being watched by a group of dolphins. Beyond the hiss and bubble sounds of her own underwater breathing she could hear a rapid clicking noise coming from the dolphins.

Four heavily-spotted dolphins peeled away from the larger group and came swimming towards her. They moved in harmony, like perfectly trained dancers. Just before they reached her, they all pointed their heads down and sank gently to the bottom. For a few moments they balanced with their noses resting in the soft, white sand. Only their tails moved, waving very slightly. Then, one by one, they shot up and circled Jody before rising back to the surface. She felt honoured and pleased by this attention. She was sure this was their way of saying 'hello' and welcoming her to their underwater world.

As they swam slowly around her, Jody was able to recognise Nebula, Dottie and Cressy. She wasn't sure about the identity of the fourth.

Looking over at her dad to check that it was OK, Jody finned after the dolphins. After a quick visit to the surface, they came back and glided beside her, two on each side. She was thrilled. They matched their speed to hers, so it felt like she was part of the group, travelling slowly through this magical, underwater world.

Everything was clear and brilliantly lit. In this sheltered, shallow bay there was no hidden danger; nowhere to hide. Gazing down, Jody tried to imagine the wreckage of a ship buried beneath mounds of gently rippled white sand. If it really had been there for nearly three hundred years, surely it was gone for good by now and would never be seen again, she thought.

When she looked up towards the surface, Jody saw four pairs of legs churning the water. She recognised the shorter, paler legs – they belonged to her brothers – and Maddie and Cam were just as easily identified. But it was certainly a strange view to have of people!

She realised she was seeing them just as the dolphins did.

Suddenly, the clicking sounds made by the dolphins, which had faded away into the background, became louder and much more intense. Jody could feel it against her eardrums. She turned, and saw three more dolphins arriving. She recognised Mary and Skipper at once. They were accompanied by another adult. All three were swimming very close together, the two adults pressed tightly against the calf as if to keep Skipper from getting away.

Happy to see her friends, Jody swam forward to greet them.

Then she stopped and stared in horror at poor little Skipper. Wrapped tightly around the baby dolphin's tail, cutting deeply into the flesh, was a fishing line. She could also see several metres of the line trailing behind him.

The three dolphins circled Jody, rising up until they were above her head. As she looked up, she saw that the tightly wrapped fishing-line was not the worst of the calf's problems. A large fish-hook was sunk into his flesh.

A lump came to Jody's throat. She felt horrified for poor little Skipper, and fearful, but she knew that wouldn't help him. She had to stay calm and keep her wits about her.

Suddenly she realised that Mary and her friend had brought Skipper to her because they knew she could help. They couldn't free the baby dolphin from the fishing-line and hook, but perhaps Jody could.

I'll try, she said to them silently, hoping they would sense her feelings. *It might hurt, but I will get it off.*

She made herself be calm, and tried to communicate that sense of calm to them. It was so important that the calf should be still while she worked on the line! If he moved suddenly she knew she might hurt him even more.

Jody sank down to kneel on the bottom. For a moment she stayed very still, waiting. Then the dolphins came down after her. The two adults guided Skipper until he was resting on the soft sand right in front of her. They stayed, one on each side, keeping him still.

Jody reached out a hand to stroke the calf's side. His round eye watched her trustingly, and he didn't move as she touched him gently. She moved her hand along his body to find the fish-hook. She felt a little sick as she saw the damage it had done. It had torn the skin, leaving a raw, jagged cut a couple of centimetres long. She knew the hook would have to be pulled out or the calf might die from an infection, or be snagged on something by the trailing line. If that happened, he could become trapped and, unable to rise to the surface for air, he would drown.

Suddenly, all three dolphins let out a chattering stream of clicks. Jody pulled her hand back and watched, bewildered, as they rose together, moving away from her, up through the water. Had she done something wrong? Had she frightened them?

Skipper in trouble!

Only when they returned, less than a minute later, did Jody understand that they'd had to go up to the surface to breathe. She knew then that she would have to work fast, and wondered if she could really do it.

But just as the dolphins arrived, so did Jody's parents, having noticed the dolphins' strange behaviour. Jody breathed a sigh of relief.

Through his mask, her father's eyes were concerned. 'Are you OK?' he signalled.

Jody pointed to herself and made the 'I'm OK' signal. Then she pointed at the baby dolphin and waved her forearm to and fro, fist clenched. This was the divers' signal meaning 'Need immediate help!'

Craig moved to get a better look at Skipper. Seeming to understand, the adult dolphins shifted their position, moving away so he could examine the calf.

Jody saw her father's lips tighten. She knew he felt as angry as she did at the careless fishermen who had let this happen. She watched as he reached for the knife which he wore in a sheath strapped to his left leg.

While Gina kept on filming, Craig used the knife to cut away the tightly wrapped fishing-line, Jody held

Skipper, stroking him gently, keeping him as calm and still as she could.

When Craig pulled away the fishing line the calf wriggled and made some high-pitched noises. Jody saw dark droplets of blood flow out of the cuts left by the line. But although what Craig was doing must have hurt, it seemed Skipper trusted him. He didn't try to get away. Mary made more clicking sounds, and Skipper calmed down.

Soon, all of the line was gone except for a short bit attached to the hook, which was still embedded in the baby dolphin's flesh. Craig grasped hold of the shaft and tried to pull it out. It moved slightly within the wound, and when that happened, the calf jumped and trembled with pain and fear. Jody held him tightly to stop him from swimming away, and heard urgent clicking noises coming from both adult dolphins. The calf settled down, although he was still trembling.

Jody looked at her father. He held up his knife. She nodded, and moved to hold the baby dolphin still, as her father operated. It was hard to watch as her father slipped the blade of the knife right into the wound, especially as Skipper was wriggling and crying out in pain. She kept on stroking him and trying to keep him calm as Craig dug the barbed hook out as quickly as he could.

Jody saw her father pull the hook free. A gout of blood, greenish in the underwater light, escaped. Craig immediately pressed down hard on the wound with his hand, holding it closed. Jody felt the baby dolphin relax. It had stopped crying and wriggling. The worst of the pain was over.

After a little while, Craig cautiously moved his hand away. The wound stayed closed and there was only a little blood now. Jody stopped holding Skipper and waited to see what the calf would do.

The little dolphin rose up slightly in the water. Mary came up close and looked at the cut where the fish-hook had been, then ran her nose all down the calf's tail, checking it out. Then she swam over to Jody and gazed at her, eye to eye. Jody felt a little shock of connection, just as if Mary had spoken to her.

All three dolphins began to swim in a circle around Jody and Craig, clicking loudly. Jody could feel the sound they made not just in her ears, but throughout her body, a warm, grateful, friendly feeling.

A moment later the dolphins were gone, racing to the surface for a much-needed breath of air, then swimming rapidly away.

7

July 26 – late.

I've been so worried about Skipper, wondering if his wound would heal OK. But now I'm happy to say that he is fine! I finally got to see him today, when a big group of dolphins came up to Honey Bee. I spotted Mary and Skipper among them.

As soon as I got into the water, Skipper swam right up and rubbed against my legs. He made it clear he wanted me to stroke him, so I did. I could hardly believe it – I was scared that he'd be nervous of me after what happened. He might have associated me with the memory of being hurt. Instead, it seemed like he wanted to thank me . . . rubbing against me like a big cat . . . just the way dolphins do with each other! He and his mother stayed close to me the whole time I was in the water.

Matt said that Mary and Skipper have accepted me as an 'honorary dolphin'! I just about burst out crying . . . does that sound silly? I was so moved . . . thinking about it now brings tears to my eyes. It isn't that I want to be a dolphin or anything like that, but to know that these wonderful creatures trust me is . . . well, I can't really find the words to express how thrilled and honoured that makes me feel.

Skipper let me check out his wound without any fuss. It looked OK to me but, just to be sure, I asked Matt what he thought. One of the guests on board was a vet, so she had a look, too. She said she didn't get many (actually, not any!) dolphins at her practice back home in Norman, Oklahoma, but her professional opinion was that the wound was healing nicely, and the scar probably won't even be noticeable after Skipper gets his grown-up spots in a few years.

Better wrap this up and get some sleep. Brittany is bound to get up early tomorrow because that's when her mother has promised to call with her exciting news . . .

'Wait'll Mommy hears that I've got my diving certification,' Brittany said breathlessly, brushing her well-brushed hair yet again. 'She won't believe it! It's funny, you know – she's not much good at sporty things herself, so she never thinks I will be, either.'

Putting the hairbrush down, she turned to look at Jody, who was sitting on the edge of the bunk, lacing up her sneakers. 'All that stuff I said about how it was going to be so easy for me . . . I was really trying to convince myself! I didn't want to admit how scared I was.'

Jody could see it was hard for Brittany to tell her this, and she gave her an encouraging smile. 'The main thing is that you did it anyway, in spite of being scared!' she said. 'And now you know how much fun it is, right?'

Brittany nodded enthusiastically. 'Yeah. You know, I hope Mommy doesn't want to take me home *too* soon . . . Anna was telling me about all the great dive-sites around here. I'd love to get the chance to check some of them out . . .'

'That would be fun,' Jody agreed. She stood up. 'Come on, let's go get some breakfast.'

'I'm too excited to eat,' Brittany objected, but she followed Jody out to the saloon. The air was fragrant with the smells of fried bacon and eggs, toast, and freshly brewed coffee. Jody's mouth watered, and she hurried up behind Maddy and Cam to get her food from Mei Lin in the galley.

As she sat down, Jody noticed the sleek, black shape of a mobile phone resting beside Harry's plate. She was just digging in to her bacon and eggs when the phone's merry little tune pealed out.

Brittany gasped, and jumped up.

Harry picked up the phone and answered it. 'Yes . . . Hello, Gail . . . yes, she's right here.' Harry handed the phone to his daughter across the table.

Jody put down her fork and crossed her fingers.

'Hello?' Brittany spoke almost timidly. Then her voice changed, becoming warm and excited. 'Mommy! Oh, Mommy, I'm so glad you called! I've missed you! Wait'll you hear what I've been doing!'

Jody relaxed and picked up her fork again, exchanging a smile with her own mother.

'Now you tell me your news,' Brittany demanded cheerfully, after explaining all about her new scuba-diving skills in a breathless rush.

In the silence that followed, Jody glanced at Brittany, and was shocked by the abrupt change in her. All happiness had drained from her face.

'*Who* wants to marry you?' Brittany demanded

down the phone. Blank disbelief gave way to a furious scowl as she heard her mother's reply. 'Jacques! You have got to be kidding! No way! I hope you told him – what do you mean you said *yes*? No! I refuse to have that creep as my stepfather! He can't live with us. I won't live with him. You can't do it! I won't let you!' Brittany's voice went sliding up the scale in anger, and her face flushed beet-red.

Suddenly she pushed herself away from the table. 'No!' she shouted into the phone. 'I won't stay here! You can't make me! You're ruining my life!'

Bad news for Brittany

Looking very concerned, Harry got up and moved towards his daughter.

Brittany flung the mobile phone at her father. 'Tell her!' she shouted. The colour had drained out of her face as abruptly as it had come, and she was now very white. 'Tell her she can't get married! Tell her she has to come back and look after me!'

Harry put the phone to his ear. 'Gail?' He spoke gruffly. 'We need to talk—' Then he looked startled. He pulled the phone away from his ear and stared at it in disbelief. 'She hung up!'

Brittany stared into space. Her lips were parted and she was panting slightly. Jody thought with concern that she looked ill, and wondered if she was about to faint.

Suddenly, Brittany charged towards the hatchway. Harry stepped forward, blocking her way. She managed to stop just short of running into him.

'I'm going out. Let me go!' she cried.

'No.' Harry spoke gently but firmly. 'You're not going anywhere just now, love. Calm down. You've had a shock. I'm going to call your mother back and have a talk with her, and then – we'll get this sorted, I promise.'

Brittany looked at her father. Then she nodded

tersely, turned on her heel and stalked out. A second later, Jody heard the sound of their cabin door being slammed shut.

July 27 – after breakfast.
This is awful!

Brittany won't talk to anyone. I tried my best, but – she's locked the cabin door – my cabin, incidentally! – and has been sulking inside for hours.

Harry got hold of his ex-wife and learned that she is planning to get married in the spring. She says that B. can go to Paris for the wedding. She thinks that by then a) Brittany will have 'come to her senses' and be happy about it, and b) they will have decided where they are going to live and sorted out a school for her. But until she is actually married, she doesn't want her daughter around . . . probably figures B. would scare off her fiancé! She told Harry that if it was absolutely impossible for B. to stay with him on Dolphin Dreamer, she would find her a good boarding school.

I feel bad for Brittany, but if I'm honest I can't stand the thought of having to put up with her until next spring! I know she has been so much nicer lately, but that's because she was enjoying her vacation. I haven't forgotten what she was like at first . . . and if she is forced to stay with us, it will be an absolute nightmare! Especially once we are at sea, with no escape . . . How many more times will I get locked out of my own cabin? I am sure Brittany would fit right in at some snobby boarding school, but Harry doesn't think so. Despite all the trouble she has been so far, he wants her to stay with him rather than pack her off to a strange school. So Mom and Dad have agreed: the twins and I are going to have home schooling (with a little help from the Internet!) from September onwards, and B. could have the same. But I could hardly believe my ears when Mom went on to say how great it was for me to have 'a friend her own age' on board. OK, I know she was trying to make Harry feel better, but honestly. *That spoiled brat my* friend?

And when Brittany has a problem, it throws a monkey-wrench into all our plans. I missed the chance to go out with Matt on Honey Bee *and now Mom and Dad are so concerned to help Harry sort this out they can't even think about anything else. Here it is nearly mid-day and we are still tied up in Port Lucaya, with no plans to go sailing, or diving, or anything today. It is all Brittany's fault!*

Jody was sitting by herself on the forward deck, hunched miserably over her diary, when a sound made her look up. She saw Brittany emerge from below, and tensed warily. But Brittany didn't notice her. Even though she'd put on make-up, Jody could tell that she'd been crying.

As Jody watched, puzzled, Brittany left the boat, swinging across to the boardwalk and then marching away, shoulders hunched, without looking back. Her face wore a hard, determined expression.

Jody stared after her, frowning. Maybe it was perfectly innocent. Brittany might be headed for the coffee-shop, or the diving school, or running an errand for her dad – but in that case why the make-up? And Brittany had been so upset this morning – Jody couldn't believe she'd calmed down yet. Something was wrong here.

What was she up to? Jody knew Brittany would probably be furious at her for following, but somebody had to look out for her. Stowing her diary in the sail locker, she got to her feet and hurried after her.

For once, the sun was not shining. The sky was heavily overcast, and there was a strong, warm wind blowing. As she felt it on her back, pushing her along, Jody thought it would be a good day for sailing – the sail would billow and fill and a boat would absolutely race along, driven by the winds which buffeted her now. What a bore, to have to stay ashore! Rigging rattled and clanked noisily, and the boats she hurried past bobbed and shifted in their berths.

Brittany had disappeared. Jody paused and wondered where to look for her. The coffee-shop or the diving school?

Then she saw *Stormrider*.

Jay was on the pier, passing shopping bags full of food and drink across to Marcus and the girls on board. Jody was about to turn away when she realised that there were three girls, not two, on board – and one of them was Brittany.

'Hey, Brittany, here's your friend,' called Jay as he noticed Jody standing and staring.

Brittany scowled. 'She's not my friend.' Turning to stare down at Jody she asked crossly, 'What do you want?'

'I'll bet she'd like to help us find the treasure,' said Ally. There was an amused, superior smile on her pretty face as she gazed down at Jody. 'Funny how everybody wants to get in on the act.' She shook her finger at Jody. 'Sorry, honey, but you'll just have to go find your own shipwreck. We're not sharing with anybody else.'

Jody shrugged impatiently. 'I don't care about that. I came to see Brittany.'

'Well, now you've seen me, you can run along,' Brittany snapped.

'Please, I need to talk to you,' Jody said urgently.

Jay leaped into the boat. 'Come on, let's get moving,' he said.

'Wait!' called Jody. 'Brittany, does your dad know where you are? Did he say you could go with these guys?'

Brittany shrugged. 'I can do what I like,' she said. 'Nobody cares about me.'

'That's not true!' Jody said, but Marcus was reving the engine now, and she didn't know if Brittany could hear her. She chewed her lip unhappily, trying to think of something else to say.

Brittany tossed her hair back and turned to murmur something to Ally. As *Stormrider* pulled away, the tall blonde girl gave her a mocking wave. Jody could only stare after them, helpless.

As she walked slowly away Jody wondered what to do. She didn't want to be a tattle-tale. Harry might not be bothered, anyway – he might even have given Brittany permission to go. Although Jody thought the whole *Stormrider* crew were obnoxious, Harry had met Heather and Ally and had let Brittany go to Freeport with them.

She was still turning it all over in her mind when she heard a familiar voice call, 'Ahoy, Jody!'

She looked up, astonished, to see the yellow sails of *Honey Bee*, and watched as Matt and Adam manoeuvred the catamaran into the slip reserved for it.

When they had docked Jody asked, 'What are you doing back? I thought you'd be out looking for dolphins today.'

'Not in this,' replied Matt with a glance at the cloudy sky.

Jody felt a clutch of apprehension in her stomach. 'Why? It's so breezy . . . isn't it good sailing weather?'

'It is right now,' he agreed. 'We made record time! But haven't you heard the forecast? Why do you suppose *Dolphin Dreamer* stayed in dock today? Harry will have heard the warnings.'

'Warnings?' she repeated weakly.

'All sailors are being told to seek shelter. There's a major tropical storm brewing. Winds of over a hundred miles per hour predicted. There's no way anyone with any sense would want to be out at sea today!'

8

There was no time to waste. Jody spun on her heel and ran away from a bemused Matt. 'Gotta go!' she called.

She ran as fast as she could back to *Dolphin Dreamer*, leapt on board, and scrambled down through the hatch.

Cam was alone in the saloon leafing through a yachting magazine while a local radio programme of reggae music played.

'Where's Harry?' Jody gasped. 'I've got to talk to him!'

'I think he's in his cabin,' Cam said calmly. 'We've got different tastes in music, you know.' He was relaxed, grinning, unaware of any problem.

Jody hurried along to the captain's cabin and rapped sharply on the door. 'Harry? Are you there?'

'Come in,' called Harry's voice.

Jody entered and saw that he was playing a computerised chess game and listening to music.

Harry took the headphones off and a worried line appeared between his eyes as he saw the anxiety on Jody's face. 'What's wrong?' he asked.

'I just saw Brittany go off on *Stormrider*,' Jody blurted out. 'They said they're going treasure-hunting,' she added. 'I don't think they realise there's a storm coming.'

Harry quickly got to his feet. 'Those young fools,' he muttered. His blue eyes searched Jody's face. 'How long ago was this?'

'I don't know . . . ten, fifteen minutes?' Jody replied. 'I should have come sooner . . . but I saw Matt coming in and stopped to talk to him. I'm sorry. I didn't know about the storm until Matt told me.'

'OK, love,' Harry said. 'None of this is your fault. Come on. We've got to make radio contact with *Stormrider* and convince them to turn around and head straight back.'

The ship's two-way radio was on, as it always was,

in the small control room. Jody knew that it was important, especially when out at sea, to hear about any potential dangers or changes in the weather. It was also vital for vessels to be able to communicate with each other, whether sending a distress call or exchanging information.

But none of Harry's attempts to raise *Stormrider* met with success.

He slammed his hand down on the chart-table in frustration. 'Why don't they respond? They must have their radio switched off!' he said angrily. 'People like that shouldn't be allowed to rent boats. They haven't a clue what they're doing . . . and they put other people in danger with their stupidity.'

Harry's next call was to alert the police and the coast guard. 'I don't suppose you have any idea where they would be headed?' He looked at Jody without much hope.

'Yes, actually I do,' Jody said, leaning forward earnestly. 'They're still looking for the wreck of the *Elvira*. I'm sure they'll be going back to that little bay where we went diving a few days ago.'

Harry sat up straighter when he heard this. 'So at least I know where I have to go.'

'You're going after them?' Jody asked.

'One way or another,' Harry said. He had a determined look on his face. 'If this was my boat, there'd be no question about it. But if your dad doesn't want to risk *Dolphin Dreamer*, I'll rent or borrow another boat. That's my little girl out there. I have to go and bring her back.'

'And I'll be there to help you,' said Jody's father.

Startled, Jody turned and saw that her dad and Matt were both standing in the doorway where they'd obviously been listening.

'We'll take *Honey Bee*,' Matt announced. He held up a hand to silence the protests from Craig and Harry.

'A catamaran like *Honey Bee* is much more stable in rough weather,' he explained swiftly. 'Also, her engine is more powerful, which is useful if it gets too fierce for sails. Plus, I know these waters like the back of my hand, so you'll want me to navigate. And finally, we can leave straight away. *Honey Bee* is ready to go.'

'You're on,' said Harry. 'Thank you.' His voice was gruff with emotion.

As soon as Cam heard what they were planning, he said he would come too. Craig turned to Jody. 'Your mother's taken the twins to the adventure playground,' he said. 'When she gets back, tell her–'

'But I want to come, too!' Jody exclaimed. She stared anxiously into her father's eyes, willing him to understand. 'I can't help feeling that I could have stopped Brittany from going, if only I'd thought of the right thing to say! Please let me help!'

Craig hesitated, then nodded his agreement. 'I'll have a quick word with Maddie, so she knows what's up. But with luck, we may be back before they are.'

Jody sighed with relief, glad to get another chance. Even though she'd been careful to hide her annoyance in the private pages of her diary, she was afraid she had added to Brittany's feelings of being unwanted.

Honey Bee was soon sailing out of Port Lucaya with a crew of five. The wind was strong, and fortunately blowing in the right direction, so they bounded swiftly over the waves. It was a fast, rough ride. Jody kept a grip on the railing and gazed at the horizon, searching for *Stormrider*. She wondered if Brittany was feeling sea-sick, and if she was wishing herself safely back in port.

To the south and west, the sky was purple-black, and Jody could see occasional jagged flashes of lightning against the heavy clouds. Luckily they were headed north. Jody kept her eyes fixed on the friendlier, lighter grey sky and hoped they would be able to outrun the storm.

Even though they were moving much faster, the journey seemed to take a lot longer than it had under the calm, clear blue sky of last week. Minutes crawled by and the ocean threw them around as they struggled on with no end in sight. Jody chewed a piece of gum given her by the sympathetic Cam, who had said it might help settle her stomach. She was soaking wet, but at least it was warm. She couldn't tell if it was raining, or if the water that drenched her was only salt spray, from the higher and higher waves that broke against the side of the boat.

'There she is!' shouted Harry suddenly.

Jody leaned out over the edge, narrowing her eyes against the wind and the sea-spray. Then she saw *Stormrider*, and was startled by how small and fragile the sleek modern launch appeared as it was tossed up and down by the green-grey waves.

'She's riding awfully low in the water,' Craig said, sounding concerned.

Harry held the loud-hailer to his mouth. 'Ahoy, *Stormrider*!' he called. 'Ahoy! Put on your radio!'

As they drew nearer, they could see no one on deck. Jody's heart lurched. For one terrifying moment she thought that the entire crew had disappeared.

Then, a couple of figures appeared, wrapped in bright waterproofs. They were carrying plastic bowls full of water, which they poured over the side. Jody frowned, puzzled by this.

'Ahoy!' Harry hailed them again. 'Are you in trouble?'

Marcus lifted a loud-hailer to his mouth. 'The bilge-pump isn't working! We're splashing around up to our ankles! Have you got a spare pump?'

Harry looked at Matt, who shook his head.

'Tell them I'll try to fix it, 'Cam suggested. 'It's probably just blocked.'

Harry raised the loud-hailer. 'Request permission to approach and board. We'll try to fix it for you!'

Jody was sure Marcus would have agreed, but Jay snatched the loud-hailer from him and shouted, 'I'll fix it myself! We don't need any help! Back off, *Honey Bee*!'

Harry lifted the loud-hailer. 'Put your radio on! There's a tropical storm warning, all boats advised to get in to port!'

'I'm not scared of storms!' Jay replied. 'We'll ride it out – this boat was made for rough seas! Don't worry about us, Grampa!'

Harry to the rescue!

Harry set his shoulders, determined to make them understand the danger. 'Winds are predicted of over a hundred miles an hour! That's more than a storm – it's practically a hurricane!'

Jay made a rude noise. 'How dumb do you think we are? It's not hurricane season yet!'

As he was speaking, Ally and Brittany appeared at the side to pour more water overboard. Brittany was wrapped in an oversized, bright yellow waterproof and didn't look happy at all. When she caught sight of *Honey Bee*, she gave a cry. Then she turned and tugged at Jay's arm, speaking urgently.

He tried to shrug her off, then spoke impatiently into the loud-hailer again. 'I guess you'd better take this little girl back with you. You'll be pleased to know you've managed to scare her!'

Harry turned to Matt, Craig and Cam, who were waiting for his orders. He spoke quietly. 'Getting close enough isn't going to be safe–'

'I'll take down the sails,' Matt said immediately, and he and the other two men got to work right away.

Harry lifted the loud-hailer again. 'Brittany – do you have a life-jacket on?'

On the other boat, Brittany nodded, and opened

the yellow waterproof to show her father she was prepared.

'Good girl,' he boomed back. 'We're going to come as close as we can, but you'll have to climb across. Could be tricky. Keep your wits about you. But don't worry, we'll get you safely home. Anyone else on *Stormrider* want to come with us?'

Brittany turned away and shouted into the cabin: 'Ally! Heather! Come with me! It's not safe here!'

Red-haired Heather, wearing a blue waterproof, popped out for a moment. 'I need help, you guys!' she shouted. 'The water's getting deeper!'

Ally tugged at Marcus' arm, pointing to his bowl, and the two of them vanished below.

Cam switched on the engine, and Matt manoeuvred *Honey Bee* alongside *Stormrider*. Handing the loud-hailer to Craig, Harry swung himself up onto the side and balanced himself there, one hand gripping the rigging.

Jody chewed her lip as she watched him. Even in calmer weather it would have been a risky position. What if he fell? She remembered how, back at the start of their journey on *Dolphin Dreamer*, an unexpected lurch of the boat in a rough sea had sent her overboard . . .

'OK, sweetheart,' Harry shouted. 'Wait till I say, and then step across to me!'

Brittany nodded.

Honey Bee lurched under the impact of a strong wave, and Harry swayed, but stayed where he was. Jody could hear Matt muttering under his breath as he grappled with the tiller, trying his best to hold the boat steady. The two boats drew closer still.

'Now!' Harry snapped. Wedging his foot between two lines, he leaned with outstretched arms. Jody held her breath. She could hardly bear to watch, but she couldn't look away. Brittany stepped off the side of *Stormrider* just as it was rocked by a wave. The gap between the two boats widened, and for a moment it seemed that the girl would plunge down into the water.

But her father grabbed hold of her, and pulled her onto *Honey Bee*, setting her down on deck. Brittany burst into tears.

Harry patted her back a little awkwardly. He looked at Jody. 'Look after her, please,' he said quietly. He turned to Craig. 'We can't leave them to drown,' he said. Then, to Jody's astonishment, he leapt back to his perch on the side, and swung himself across to the other boat. They heard Jay give an angry yell as he landed.

Brittany screamed. 'Daddy!'

Jody grabbed her, afraid she would try to go after her father. She stared across and saw Harry vanish into the hold, despite Jay's protests.

'If somebody doesn't fix that pump, *Stormrider*'s sunk,' Cam explained.

'It may be too late already,' Matt said, standing grimly at the helm, trying to keep the boats close without colliding. The waves were getting higher and higher; Jody felt as if someone was pouring buckets of water onto them, and she was dizzy from the pitching of the boat.

'You girls had better get below,' Craig said.

'Not without my daddy,' Brittany said with a catch in her voice.

Craig didn't reply. His face was very pale and still. Jody had never seen her father look like that. She realised he was frightened. Suddenly, she was terrified. What if it was too late – not only for *Stormrider*, but for all of them on board *Honey Bee* as well?

The boat pitched wildly. Jody felt her stomach drop, as if she was on a roller-coaster, and she grabbed at the side to steady herself. The sea lifted them up. They were above *Stormrider*. The motorboat seemed to nestle in the hollow of the wave. Then the movement of the sea brought *Honey Bee* down again, and a wave closed over *Stormrider*.

Sturdy *Honey Bee* found her balance again. But *Stormrider* wallowed. Before Jody's horrified gaze, the launch began to sink.

They could hear cries of fear from *Stormrider*'s crew. Jody and Brittany leaned forward together, holding on to each other, peering anxiously at the other deck, searching for Harry on the foundering vessel.

Cam lifted the loud-hailer to his mouth. 'Harry! Are you all right? Ahoy, *Stormrider*! Abandon ship!'

Matt brought his boat closer. There was a loud, grinding shriek as it scraped against the other boat's hull, and he winced. 'Get ropes and life-jackets,' he shouted to Craig. 'Some of those fools aren't wearing them!'

'Take it easy.' Harry's voice, amazingly calm and reassuring, boomed out from the loud-hailer on the half-submerged boat. 'We're all OK. Help us aboard, one at a time.'

Jody grabbed her father's arm. 'Can I do anything to help?' she asked.

Craig shook his head, not taking his eyes from the other boat. 'I don't think so. You and Brittany look after yourselves and keep out of the way.'

She let go of him reluctantly. She wondered if it would be safer down below, but couldn't bear to miss anything.

It gave her a strange, sick feeling to see *Stormrider* lying half-submerged, battered by waves which seemed determined to drag the boat under. Her crew were clinging on to whatever they could, and crying out for help. Only Harry, standing on deck waist-deep in water, seemed in control. Jody was amazed by how brave he was.

She had to clamp her jaws together to stop her teeth chattering as she saw her father climb up and balance himself on the side of the boat. He was wearing a life-jacket, and had a rope tied around his waist. Cam was hanging on to the rope to keep him from being pulled in along with the people he was trying to save.

Ally was the first person to come aboard. Her long blonde hair hung in dripping rattails around her face. Her teeth were chattering and her eyes were round and staring with shock. Moments later, Heather, shaking and weeping, joined her.

Jody cried out as she saw her father stumble and

almost tumble down into the sea. But Cam had a firm grip on the rope he held, and pulled him back to safety. A few moments later, with Matt's help, they hauled the heavy Marcus on board. A minute or so later, Jay, the last member of the crew, had been saved. Only then did Harry clamber across to safety with Craig's help, out of breath and red-faced, but smiling reassuringly at Brittany.

She moaned and flung herself into his arms. 'Oh, Daddy, Daddy, I was so scared!'

Jody, hugging her own dad, was startled by his reply.

'So was I, love,' Harry murmured, holding his daughter tightly. 'Scared to death, I was. But we're OK. We're OK.'

Matt shouted above the wind and rain. 'Cam, give me a hand to batten everything down! Everybody else, get below now!'

The next hour was one of the longest of Jody's life. They all huddled below deck and waited for the storm to pass. She couldn't stop thinking about *Stormrider* sinking beneath the waves; how quickly the boat had filled with water, and how impossible it had been to stop. What if that happened to them? But *Honey Bee* was a sturdy boat, snug and sound. The only seawater inside was that dripping off everybody's wet clothes.

The *Stormrider* crew kept to themselves at the far end of the cabin, muttering and complaining together. Matt offered them towels, food and drink, then left them alone. He began swapping sea-stories with Cam and Harry. Their descriptions of comic sailing mishaps and near-disasters took Jody's mind off what was happening outside. Even Brittany stopped shivering and perked up a little to listen to her dad.

The worst moment was when they felt a huge crashing bang right above them which shook the whole boat. Jody gave a yelp of fright, and felt her father's arm tighten around her reassuringly.

'Sounds like the mast is down,' said Harry.

Matt was already on his feet. 'I'll just check that it didn't block the hatchway,' he said. He was back a few moments later, to report that the broken mast had fallen clear of the door, and that the storm did finally seem to be passing.

Ten minutes later, he was back at the helm with the engine running, and *Honey Bee* was heading for home.

9

July 28 – late.

The Stormrider *crew is just unbelievable! Except for Heather – who insisted on giving everybody – but especially Harry and Matt – big kisses when she left! – they didn't seem at all grateful to be saved. Marcus complained because there wasn't any beer on board. None of them think what happened was their fault at all. Jay just talked about suing the charter company for giving him a defective boat.*

Hopefully we have seen the last of them.

Brittany has gone to the other extreme. She has apologised to everybody for causing so much trouble. She hangs around like a sad little ghost, all pale and quiet. She keeps offering to do things for people. It seems she can't stand to be alone for a minute. If she is not following her dad, then she's trailing after Maddie, or Mom – or me! Yeah, that's the worst thing. She's always trying to be nice to me now. She says it's because I saved her life. I told her it wasn't me, it was Harry and Matt she had to thank, but she insisted that it was all down to me. If I hadn't followed her, and then gone to tell Harry, he wouldn't have known to go after her, and she would have drowned. They all would have drowned.

This may sound weird, but I kind of miss the old, selfish Brittany . . .

'And one more for Jody,' said Brittany, putting the last blueberry muffin onto Jody's plate. Usually everyone lined up to get their own food from the galley, but this morning Brittany had insisted on serving.

Jimmy scowled. 'That's not fair!'

'Thanks, but I don't need two,' Jody replied. She lobbed it across the table to her brother. 'You guys can split it,' she said, to stop any argument.

'Why are you being so nice to Jody?' Sean demanded.

'Because she saved my life,' said Brittany, turning to smile at Jody.

Jody shrugged her shoulders uncomfortably and stared down at her plate. She wished Brittany would stop saying that.

'That's a heavy burden to put on Jody's shoulders, Brittany,' said Mei Lin, slipping into the last place at the big table.

'What do you mean?' Brittany frowned uncertainly. 'I just want to be nice to her.'

'In China we believe that if you save someone's life, you become responsible for that person forever after,' Mei Lin explained.

Jody felt the hairs on the back of her neck prickle. She stared at Brittany and saw the other girl's gaze reflect back her uneasiness. Obviously Brittany didn't like that idea any more than she did!

Harry suddenly spoke up. 'I rather think that Brittany is *my* responsibility,' he said firmly, but with a warm look across the table at his daughter.

Brittany nodded, flushing slightly. 'I – I know. I didn't mean – I just wanted everybody to know – I know what I did was wrong, and–'

'But just think,' Jody interrupted as the thought occurred to her, 'if you *hadn't* gone off on

Stormrider, those guys would all have drowned!
Nobody would have gone after them. So, in a way,
you saved *their* lives!'

Brittany stared back at her, her eyes very round.
Finally, she found her tongue. 'Well, in that case, I'm
glad we don't all live in China!'

Just as they were finishing breakfast, Matt arrived
with a tall, slender, fair-haired couple, who
looked so much alike they were obviously brother
and sister.

'These are my friends, Alex and Ismay Collins,' he
said.

Jody remembered the names. 'Are you the treasure-
hunters?' she asked.

Alex flashed a grin. 'Yes . . . but we haven't had
much luck so far this summer. So, today we are doing
some better-paid salvage work. The owners have hired
us to find *Stormrider*, recover her if possible, and
prepare a report for the insurers, if not.'

'And since you all saw it sink,' Matt said, 'I thought
maybe you'd be willing to help Alex and Ismay locate
the wreck. I'm going to be too busy myself with the
repairs to *Honey Bee*.'

Brittany spoke up. 'What happened to Jay and – I

mean, what about the people who rented the boat? Couldn't they help?'

Ismay made a face. 'Maybe, if they'd stuck around. But it seems they cut their holiday short and took the first available flight home, rather than stay and explain what happened.'

Brittany scowled. 'Cowards,' she muttered.

Jody agreed. It was typical of them to think nothing of the damage they were doing, and leave it to others to clean up afterwards.

'What do you want us to do, exactly?' Craig asked. 'I mean, obviously Matt could show you on a chart roughly where she went down . . .'

'True,' agreed Alex with a nod. 'And maybe it will be a simple thing to find her straight away. But maybe not. That storm will have churned and shifted the sand, and the boat may have broken up. The more people out looking, the more quickly we should find her. Matt tells us you dive?'

Jody caught her breath with excitement. She could hardly believe it. She checked, to make sure she hadn't misunderstood: 'You want us to dive with you?'

Ismay's eyebrows went up. She looked apprehensive. 'Only if you'd like to come along. I understand from Matt that the boat went down in an area where you've been diving before, so you'll be familiar with it. It's shallow, and the visibility should be good today. We wouldn't expect you to do any actual work, and we can't afford to pay you . . .'

Craig burst out laughing. 'I think Jody would be prepared to pay *you* for the chance!' he said, when he could manage to speak. 'Thanks for the invitation – we would love to come along and help you look for *Stormrider*!'

Craig, Gina, Jody and Brittany quickly collected their diving gear and everything else they would need for a day's dive. Harry said he'd go along to provide back-up support on board. Sean and Jimmy were happy to stay behind with Maddie and Cam, after making their parents promise to tell them if they came across any sunken pirate ships.

'If we do, we'll get it all on videotape, I promise you,' Craig said solemnly before waving goodbye and heading off to board *New Treasure Seeker*, Alex and Ismay's sturdy salvage vessel.

They soon reached the bay where *Stormrider* had gone down.

Brittany seemed startled when Alex cut the engine and dropped anchor. 'Is this really the same place?'

she asked, staring around in bewilderment.

Jody guessed she was remembering the slate-grey, storm-lashed sea beneath a purple sky. That terrifying vision had disappeared, replaced by calm breezes under a bright blue sky which now arched over crystal clear waters. Staring down to the sea-bed – only about eight metres away – Jody thought that the smooth white sand looked as if it had rested undisturbed for centuries. But that was an illusion. The sands were always being moved and shifted by the weather, which could change in a matter of hours from calm to deadly.

There were still a few bits of litter from *Stormrider* bobbing about on the waves – the styrofoam lid of a cool-box, a red plastic bowl, empty beer cans – but there was no sign of the launch itself. It had completely vanished.

Jody noticed that Brittany was shivering, despite the warmth of the day. Harry was watching her with concern.

'Why don't you stay here with me, love?' he suggested. 'I'll tell you some more sea-stories.' He smiled, trying to coax a response out of her.

She shook her head, staring out at the blue water. 'No, I want to dive,' she said quietly. 'I hate the thought of seeing *Stormrider* down there . . . but I have to do it.'

Harry nodded slowly. 'That's up to you,' he replied.

After they were all ready and their equipment had been checked, they paired off and discussed their dive plans. Jody's buddy would be her father, while Gina would look after the less-experienced Brittany.

'Remember, I'll be right beside you,' Gina told Brittany, her brown eyes soft and concerned. 'I'm sure there won't be any problems. But if you feel uncomfortable, or tired, or want to come up again for any reason at all, just signal, and we'll end the dive.'

'Thanks, Mrs McGrath,' Brittany said.

Gina smiled. 'Why don't you call me Aunt Gina?' she suggested. 'You could be my honorary niece! I've just about given up on my sister ever giving me a niece or nephew . . .'

To Jody's surprise, this suggestion brought a flush of pleasure to Brittany's pale face, and she smiled shyly as she said, 'Thanks . . . Aunt Gina!'

Once in the water, Jody descended two or three metres, keeping pace with her father. Gentle kicks with her fins propelled her smoothly through the water. Craig, who had the camera today, went more slowly, and Jody soon outdistanced him. They had agreed beforehand that this was OK, as long as she didn't go out of sight. Visibility was so good in this clear water that Jody was sure this wouldn't be a problem.

It did seem puzzling that they had not managed to spot *Stormrider* yet. How could it just disappear, in such shallow water? She wondered if they were wrong about the spot. Maybe the floating litter that had seemed like a marker was misleading. It might have drifted away much farther than they realised. Without permanent landmarks, it was hard to know where you were at sea.

Jody's attention was distracted from the search when she caught sight of a group of dolphins. She swam towards them. Two peeled away from the group and glided rapidly towards her.

Even at a distance Jody could see that one was an adult, heavily spotted, and the other, smaller, just a calf. They came closer still and, with a joyful leap of her heart, Jody recognised Mary and Skipper.

The calf zoomed right up to her and rubbed affectionately against Jody's side. He swam around her quickly several times and then darted away back to his mother.

Mary swam closer to Jody. Jody could hear her

clicking. Then she flipped over and glided away a short distance before swimming back again, circling Jody and again gliding away slowly, waving her tail in a beckoning way.

Jody had the strong feeling that the dolphin wanted her to follow. She looked around for her father and saw that he had the video camera pointed in their direction – he had seen the whole thing. She pointed to indicate she wanted to follow Mary. He nodded and signalled OK.

Jody swam after Mary and Skipper. She was a little apprehensive that Mary might be taking her to rescue another injured dolphin. Yet Mary's clicking sounds and her whole body language seemed to promise something very different this time.

They went deeper. Jody realised they were heading for the group of dolphins, who were hovering in the water with their noses down. Jody thought they were looking at something on the seabed. As she drew nearer, she could see that it was something quite large sticking up out of the sand . . . something like the hull of a ship! Yes, it was definitely a wreck!

Jody finned harder, excited by the thought that she'd been the first to spot *Stormrider*. But she was puzzled because what was lying there before her, half-covered by the shifting sands, didn't look anything like the modern launch she remembered. Two days at the bottom of the sea shouldn't have changed it that much. She swam closer, trying to make sense of what she was looking at, searching for a detail she could focus on.

The curious dolphins parted before her like a curtain, letting her through, and now she saw what they had been looking at.

Thrusting up out of the sands was the head and upper body of a woman. Not a real woman, but a statue carved of wood, a face with wide open eyes, a straight nose and smiling lips.

Jody reached out one hand and touched the old ship's figurehead wonderingly. She couldn't quite believe it, but, as she felt the ancient wood solid and real beneath her fingers, she knew it was true. Thanks to the dolphins, she'd discovered an ancient shipwreck.

While Jody was busy with her discovery, Alex and Ismay had found *Stormrider*, still in one piece. The next step should have been to haul the launch to the surface and tow it in to port. But when they heard Jody's exciting news, back on board the *New*

Elvira, at last!

Treasure Seeker, they decided that could wait.

'It must be *Elvira*!' Ismay exclaimed.

'If it's not, it must be something just as good,' Alex added. 'You wouldn't believe how many times we've been diving in this very spot, and never found a thing!'

'I guess we have the storm to thank for uncovering it,' Ismay said with a grin.

'No, you have the dolphins to thank,' Jody put in.

'They're the ones who led me to it!'

'Honestly, Jody, you have to drag dolphins into *everything*,' Brittany groaned.

Jody looked at her sharply, but was that a twinkle in Brittany's eye? Maybe she was teasing. 'Oh, I don't know,' Jody replied lightly. 'I think in this case I'd say it was the dolphins who dragged *me* into it.'

'And are we ever glad they did!' said Alex enthusiastically. 'Do you guys need to rest, or are you up for a little treasure-hunting?'

'Treasure-hunting, definitely!' Jody exclaimed. She shot a pleading look at her parents and was relieved to see they looked nearly as excited as she felt.

'Yeah, count me in!' Brittany agreed. She had obviously recovered her nerve, Jody thought.

'I think we could manage another dive, after a short rest,' said Craig, a huge grin on his face.

Gina sounded a note of caution. 'At least another hour before we dive again,' she said. 'And we'll have to set a strict time-limit. I know how easy it is to get carried away and forget everything else when exploring something as exciting as this!'

'Sure,' said Alex. 'I suggest a dive of three-quarters of an hour. We'll take a look, and bring up any interesting small objects that we find. Everything else will have to wait for another day. After all, we still have to do the job we're being paid for, and haul up *Stormrider*!'

While *New Treasure Seeker* was being moved so that she would sit in the water immediately above the wreck of *Elvira*, Gina reminded the girls of the importance of keeping their wits about them. 'Stay in constant visual contact with the rest of us. Don't go diving into any enclosed areas unless one of us has checked it out first, and be careful where you put your hands. Eels have a tendency to make their homes in wrecks, and if you disturb one you could get a nasty bite,' she said.

'Anna warned me about camouflaged fish like stonefish and scorpion fish that have poisonous stings,' Brittany said. 'Don't worry, Aunt Gina, I'll be careful. I don't intend to grab anything unless it's made of gold or silver!'

Gina laughed. 'We should be so lucky!' she said.

'But you are that lucky!' Alex exclaimed exuberantly, with a grin that seemed to split his face in two. 'We're all that lucky! Today is our lucky day!'

The dolphins were still hovering around the old wreck. They seemed fascinated by what the storm winds had uncovered. The normally smooth, sandy bottom they knew had been transformed.

As she approached the site with the others, Jody was so excited she had to remind herself to breathe normally through her regulator.

Only a part of the ship had been uncovered by the shifting sands; most of it remained buried. As she swam closer, Jody tried to figure out which part of the ship she was looking at, and where any treasure was most likely to be. Could there still be a locked chest hidden away on board? Or would its contents have been scattered far and wide long before now? Her eyes scanned the sea-bed as she hoped to catch the gleam of gold or silver.

Jody saw the others busily fanning the sand with their gloved hands to uncover objects hidden there. She tried it herself, but found only more sand. She looked around at the others again and saw that they were all making discoveries, tucking found objects safely into the mesh collecting-bags which Alex had handed out before the dive.

Ismay held up something flat and round, the size of a dinner plate. Craig was inspecting some lumpy object, and Alex's bag was already bulging. Even Brittany had made a discovery. Jody swam closer to look, and the other girl huddled protectively over her find. Jody thought the tiny things she was picking up looked like a bunch of pebbles, not interesting at all. Anyway, it was clear that Brittany didn't want to share them with her. She'd better find her own place to look.

Jody noticed something like a bottle sticking out of the sand, but decided against it. Bottles were boring. She wanted to find something better! So she continued to search.

Yet when she saw her mother signal ten minutes to go, Jody was still empty-handed.

She gazed around, despairing, and noticed Mary and Skipper were close by, watching her curiously. Jody was startled to realise that she'd been too preoccupied with her search to pay any attention to the dolphins – that had to be a first! All of a sudden, she felt annoyed with herself for letting the treasure-hunting fever overwhelm her like that. She'd been the first to spot the wreck. That should be enough.

She was sorry now that she hadn't just relaxed and played with Mary and Skipper. She swam towards them eagerly, determined to make it up to them in the few minutes she had left.

With a flick of her tail, Mary shot away, her calf

swimming rapidly beneath her. A moment later, Mary doubled back to be sure Jody was following. She slowed down, letting the girl catch up. Then she did a somersault, ending by balancing on her nose in the soft white sand.

Jody wasn't sure what this game was, but she decided to imitate the dolphin. She shot down to the bottom and attempted a handstand there. As her fingers closed on the soft bed, she felt something hard and flat beneath the sand. Digging down a little deeper, she managed to hook her fingers into something and pull it up.

Looking at her find she saw that it was a dark, metallic disc, slightly bigger than her outstretched hand. Jody felt a moment's flare of excitement – that she'd *finally* found something – followed immediately by disappointment. It was man-made, and it *could* have come from the shipwreck, but whatever it might be, it wasn't treasure! It was something like a wheel or cog; it probably came from some sort of machine or engine. And if so, then it didn't belong to the *Elvira* at all. It might even have dropped off *Stormrider*.

She nearly dropped it back into the sand. But then she stopped herself. Whatever it was, it didn't belong in the ocean. She stowed it away in her collecting bag, and then finned alongside Mary and Skipper until she received the signal to return.

10

'Anyone find any gold or valuable jewels?' Ismay asked with a smile when they'd all gathered back on deck.

They all laughed and shook their heads.

'No, me neither,' Ismay said cheerfully. 'I haven't found any serious treasure yet, but I am absolutely certain that it's down there. Have a look at this!' From her collecting bag she pulled out two large discs made of some pitted and corroded greyish metal.

'What are those?' Brittany asked.

'Dinner plates,' Ismay replied, smiling. 'I think they're made of pewter, rather than silver, but they were marked with the ship's name, probably to discourage anyone from walking off with them. Look!' She rubbed the side of her hand hard against the flat rim and then held the plate up on display.

They all crowded close to see.

Jody read the name etched in curving letters on the raised rim: 'Elvira!'

'Yes,' said Alex, smiling as widely as his sister. 'So there can be no doubt about it – we have definitely found the ship we've been searching for these past three years!'

'Anyone else want a drink?' Ismay asked. She gave the plate to her brother and went to open the cooler. 'I'm parched!' She began to hand out soft drinks and bottled water.

Jody gulped down an orangeade thirstily.

'So what happens next?' Craig wanted to know. 'Will you be able to stake a claim, or will it become a free-for-all, with lots of treasure-hunting divers turning up?'

'It would be best if we can keep the news to ourselves for as long as we can,' Alex said cautiously.

'Don't worry – we won't tell anyone,' Jody assured him.

Brittany snorted. 'Not even your nosey kid brothers?' she asked.

Craig raised his eyebrows. 'We'll tell the twins it's a secret. They won't want any bad guys beating our friends to the treasure!' he assured her.

'We will probably have to hire some more divers to help us – when treasure is involved, it's best to work as quickly as possible,' Alex said.

'Especially with hurricane season coming,' Ismay added. Finishing her water, she stowed the empty bottle back in the cooler.

'We'll apply for a salvage claim from the Bahamian government,' Alex explained. 'We've had them before, so there shouldn't be any problem. What happens is, we register our intent to salvage *Elvira* – since we've found something with that name on it. Then we dive and search like loonies and hope to make our fortunes before the weather changes!'

'Could we help you look?' Brittany asked suddenly. Her eyes were bright, her cheeks flushed. Jody thought that this was the first time she had seen her looking happy since before the phone call from her mother.

'So you want to be a treasure-seeker, too, do you?' asked Ismay. She smiled sympathetically at Brittany, then looked at Craig and Gina. 'We certainly wouldn't say no to more help . . .'

145

Craig and Gina exchanged a glance before nodding.

'We'll be sticking around for at least another week or two to help Matt out,' Craig explained. 'I've already told him that *Dolphin Dreamer* is his to command while *Honey Bee* is laid up. He's got insurance to cover the repairs, but it wouldn't be fair if he had to miss out a couple of weeks at the height of the season!'

'And luckily, there are plenty of dolphins around here to study,' Gina added. 'After what Matt told us about dolphins and divers, I would really like to film the dolphins watching you while you work. I think it could make a fascinating project . . .' She broke off with a grin. 'If I don't get too distracted by the treasure myself, that is! Hey, I haven't shown you all what I found!'

Reaching into her own bag, Gina pulled out a handful of blackened spoons and forks. 'Silverware!'

'Probably the closest thing to treasure we found today,' Ismay said. 'Those should polish up very nicely, and then you could use them to eat off the plates!'

'We obviously stumbled into the pirate's dining-room,' Craig joked, displaying his own finds – two old bottles, and what might have been a cup, all heavily encrusted.

'I found a bottle, too,' said Brittany. 'And there's

these . . .' She held out her cupped hand. Jody saw that what she had taken for pebbles underwater were actually blue beads.

'A necklace!' Ismay exclaimed. 'Or possibly a rosary. Impossible to know now what they were when they were strung. They're really lovely! Clever you, to find something so small!' She looked at Jody. 'What about you, Jody? What did you find?'

Jody felt embarrassed to show them what was obviously just some bit of machinery that had dropped off a modern boat. She shrugged. 'Nothing.'

'Nothing at all?' Ismay looked surprised. 'Really? You didn't find anything at all?'

Jody shook her head, feeling herself blush. 'Well,' she said. 'I did find something, but . . . it was just some piece of a machine, I think,' she added, with a shrug.

'Did you leave it behind?' asked Alex.

'No, I brought it up,' Jody replied. 'Well, I figured, it's not important, but leaving it was like leaving litter behind,' she explained. She reached into her bag and got out the metal disc which she handed over to Alex. 'There, see? It probably just fell off some boat that was passing . . .' her voice trailed off as she took in the way Alex was examining her find. He looked genuinely interested – excited even.

Craig leaned over to investigate. 'What is it?' he asked. 'It looks very old . . .'

'It *is* very old,' Alex agreed. His voice was solemn. 'And it's complete. If this didn't come from *Elvira* then it must have come from an even earlier ship.'

'But what *is* it?' Jody asked.

'It's a bronze astrolabe,' Alex replied. 'It's very rare.'

Everyone stared at him blankly – except Ismay, who was nodding wisely.

A real find, after all!

'Clear as mud,' Craig grumbled. 'Have mercy on us ordinary folk and explain, please!'

Alex laughed. 'Sorry,' he said. 'No reason why you'd know what an astrolabe was – nobody has used them for hundreds of years!'

He went on, 'It's an early navigation tool. It works a little bit like a portable sundial.' He held up the flat disc so they could see. 'This little piece in the middle can be moved, like the hand on a clock. By pointing it in the direction of the sun, or the brightest star at night, and working out how far it was from the horizon, you can figure out the local time, and roughly where you are.'

Jody stared at him, open-mouthed. She could hardly believe what she was hearing. To think, she had nearly tossed it away! Finally she found her voice. 'So it was a good find?'

Alex grinned widely. 'You could say that,' he replied. 'In fact, it's a brilliant find – a museum piece! I know of only one other like it in this part of the world! Wait'll we get it cleaned up, and you'll see!'

August 7
Lucky seven! Today, the New Treasure Seekers struck gold! Alex and Ismay found the pirates' hoard – a great

pile of jewellery, gold chains, gold bars, gold and silver coins . . . Sean and Jimmy are absolutely ecstatic about the genuine pieces of eight that Dad brought up for them. We each get to keep one as a souvenir of our stay here . . .

Alex and Ismay wanted to give us something more to thank us. They offered to contribute to the funding of Dolphin Universe. *But we talked it over as a team and had a better idea. Since the treasure comes from here, it should help the dolphins that live in this area. Matt is doing as much as he can on his own. With more funding, he could set up a project to encourage more responsible tourism in the area, and educate people about preserving the local ecology, and not endangering the lives of the animals who live here – especially dolphins!*

We will be leaving soon, now that Honey Bee *is all ship-shape again. I went for a swim this evening with Mary and Skipper and the others. It may have been for the last time, but I hope not. Surely we'll meet again. I hope they will always remember me. No matter how many more dolphins I come to know, I'm sure I will never forget them!*

You will find lots more about dolphins on these websites:

The Whale and Dolphin Conservation Society
www.wdcs.org

International Dolphin Watch
www.idw.org

Look out for more titles in the Dolphin Diaries series:

Book 1: ***Into the Blue***

Lucy Daniels

Jody McGrath's dolphin dreams are coming true! Her whole family is sailing around the world, researching dolphins – and Jody is recording all their exciting adventures in her Dolphin Diaries...

Jody can't believe her dolphin voyage has begun. A whole world of discovery awaits her aboard *Dolphin Dreamer*. But an unexpected passenger threatens to spoil the trip of a lifetime. And when a sudden storm puts Jody's life in danger, who can she turn to for help?

Look out for more titles in the Dolphin Diaries series:

Book 2: ***Touching the Waves***

Lucy Daniels

Jody McGrath's dolphin dreams are coming true! Her whole family is sailing around the world, researching dolphins – and Jody is recording all their exciting adventures in her Dolphin Diaries . . .

The McGraths are in Key West, Florida, visiting a very special dolphin centre – with dolphin teachers! Jody loves watching the dolphins at work. But then one of the teachers goes missing . . .

Look out for more titles in the Dolphin Diaries series:

Book 4: ***Under the Stars***

Lucy Daniels

Jody McGrath's dolphin dreams are coming true! Her whole family is sailing around the world, researching dolphins – and Jody is recording all their exciting adventures in her Dolphin Diaries . . .

Jody and the rest of the crew of Dolphin Dreamer are on course for the Caribbean. Here they'll be visiting more old friends of the McGraths, but this time, Jody will get to see dolphins being born! But there's heartache as well as happiness in store . . .

ORDER FORM

0 340 77857 1	INTO THE BLUE	£3.99 ❏
0 340 77858 X	TOUCHING THE WAVES	£3.99 ❏
0 340 78495 4	UNDER THE STARS	£3.99 ❏

All Hodder Children's books are available at your local bookshop, or can be ordered direct from the publisher. Just tick the titles you would like and complete the details below. Prices and availability are subject to change without prior notice.

Please enclose a cheque or postal order made payable to *Bookpoint Ltd*, and send to: Hodder Children's Books, 39 Milton Park, Abingdon, OXON OX14 4TD, UK.
Email Address: orders@bookpoint.co.uk

If you would prefer to pay by credit card, our call centre team would be delighted to take your order by telephone. Our direct line *01235 400414* (lines open 9.00 am–6.00 pm Monday to Saturday, 24 hour message answering service). Alternatively you can send a fax on *01235 400454*.

TITLE		FIRST NAME		SURNAME	
ADDRESS					
DAYTIME TEL:			POST CODE		

If you would prefer to pay by credit card, please complete:
Please debit my Visa/Access/Diner's Card/American Express (delete as applicable) card no:

Signature ....Expiry Date: ....

If you would NOT like to receive further information on our products please tick the box. ❏